Praise for Rae Bryant

"Rae Bryant's stories yank at you over and over, desperate to give you the clue you never had and to point you, by what's left out, to a spot on this good earth where the heart might flourish. Getting there is your business, she seems to say, and she doesn't hold out much hope of your arrival, or of hers. Is it fun? Not so much. Is it necessary? Absolutely."
—Frederick Barthelme

"Rae Bryant's fiction is smart and sexy and post-feminist and dangerous and akin to doing the tango with a succubus. Do you feel lucky? Part Hannah Tinti, part Kim Addonizio—with enough intense characters, flashy dreams, and edgy visions to entangle your heart and skull for eons. Bite into these thorny stories, before they sink their teeth into you." —Richard Peabody, Editor, *Gargoyle Magazine*

"Reading Rae Bryant can be a harrowing experience; hers is a harsh world without wrong or right. But as you make your way through, pains and pleasures meet and build, until it's like drowning in a lake of silver light." —Ben Loory, Author of *Stories for Nighttime and Some for the Day* and "The TV," *The New Yorker*

Rae Bryant's fiction is rich with sensual detail, its surface clamoring for our attention like the glamoured skin of a new lover, everything fresh, everything undulled by long familiarity. And what waits beneath, begging to be revealed? Perhaps a writer striking poses, alternately a seductress, a tease, a joker, or perhaps a trickster: for while Bryant is always sure to show us a good time, there comes a sense that sometimes she's making us laugh just

so we don't notice what else she's doing, the way her fingernails dig deeply at our freshest wounds, aiming to free the many splinters stuck beneath our skin, and also that oh so good pain waiting just below.
—Matt Bell, author of *How They Were Found*

"Addictive; the rawness, messiness, unattractive infection of love that can cause a woman to gnaw off her arm to sneak away from her sleeping lover. It's no surprise to find, among these stories, a new Wonder Woman, with a whip. Ah, you say: of course." —Karen Heuler, author of *Journey to Bom Goody*, recipient of the O'Henry Award

"Will make you simultaneously laugh and cringe at the squeamish awkwardness of post-one night stand intimacies...witty...strangely fantastical and familiar."
—*Flavorpill*

"If I had to describe Rae Bryant's collection *The Indefinite State of Imaginary Morals* in two words, the words would be these: damn impressive." —*Outsider Writers Collective and Press*

"*The Indefinite State of Imaginary Morals* commands attention. Bryant's observations on the arcana of the mundane—life, sex, a sense of being—are matched only by her ability to render them strange. Alternatively lyrical and minimal, these stories exemplify the capabilities of the literary weird mode. A must read for any student of post-millennial fiction." —Darin Bradley, Author of *Noise*

"Bryant creates a vivid portrayal of what it means to be human, in its gritty glory." —*Weave Magazine*

"A distinctive collection that's imaginative and compelling. These stories show the enormous talent of

Rae Bryant beginning to take hold." —Tim Wendel, author of *Castro's Curveball* and *High Heat*

"Deadpan, visceral, sharply funny." —Julie Innis

"A new genealogy of morals… a madcap ride through a land of errant desire and lost time." —Gary Percesepe, editor, *BLIP Magazine* (formerly *Mississippi Review*)

"Sweetly erotic without going over the top." —Jared Randall, *Apocryphal Road Code*

"Innovative, daring, original writing." —Kathy Fish, author of *A Peculiar Feeling of Restlessness*

Rae Bryant

The Indefinite State of Imaginary Morals

To Marie,
So good to meet
you!
Rae Bryant,
rae@raebryant.
com

Patasola Press

if words were sirens...
www.patasolapress.org

The Indefinite State of Imaginary Morals

Stories by Rae Bryant

Patasola Press
New York

Patasola Press
Brooklyn, New York

Grateful acknowledgement is made to original journals of
publication
and to artist Gustav Klimt as is listed in this collection.

ISBN: *978-0615496962*
First printing.

Cover art: Gustav Klimt, *Jurisprudence*, c. 1903.

patasolapress.org
raebryant.com

Printed in the United States of America

Acknowledgements

"[Jeezus] Changed My Oil Today," *Opium Magazine*, January 2011

Allegorie der Skulptur. Allegory of Sculpture. Gustav Klimt. 1889.

"All You Bad Sinners," *decomP*, October 2010

"Buttercrisp," *Pear Noir!* Issue 4, Summer 2010

"Chinchillas in the Air," *Annalemma*, 2010

Chor der Paradiesengel. Choir of Heavenly Angels. Detail from Beethoven Fries. Gustav Klimt. 1902.

"Collecting Calliope," *Weave Magazine* Issue 4, Spring/Summer 2010

Danae. Gustav Klimt. c. 1907

Die Leiden der Schwachen Menscheit. The Suffering of Weak Humanity. Gustav Klimt. 1902.

"Emperatriz de la Orilla del Río," *PANK*, December 2010

"Featherbedding," *Kill Author*, Vladimir Nabokov Issue 8, 2010

"Fifty Years in Halves," *Word Riot*, February 2010

Fischblut. Fish Blood. 1898.

"Fly Fishing In Neoprene Legs," *Foliate Oak Literary Magazine*," March 2010

Gorgonen. Gorgon. Gustav Klimt. 1902.

Gustav Klimt. *Goldfische. Goldfish.* Gustav Klimt. c. 1901.

Hoffnung. Hope. Gustav Klimt. 1903.

"I Keep a Vine Woven Basket by the Front Door," *A capella Zoo* Issue 4, Spring 2010

"Intolerable Impositions," *Bartleby Snopes*, Issue 4, 2010

"Monk Man and Moonshine," *Menda City Review*, Issue 16, May 2010

Nagender Kummer. Gnawing Pain. Detail from Beethoven Fries. Gustav Klimt. 1902.

"Paddlehead," *Caper Literary Journal* Issue 4, May 2010

"Postfeminist Zombie Assassins Wear Wonder Woman Underoos," *The Medulla Review* 4.1, 2010

"Solipsy Street," *Metazen*, November 2010

"Stage Play in Five Acts of Her: Matinee," *BLIP Magazine*, Summer 2010

Stehende alte Frau im Profil nach links. Staying Old Woman. Gustav Klimt. Date Unknown.

Stehender Mädchenakt mit vorgebeugten Körper nach links. Staying Female Nude with Bended Body Heading Left. Gustav Klimt. Date Unknown.

"Stiletto Dance," *Foundling Review*, April 2010

"Street Red," *Writer's Bloc* (Rutgers-Camden), 2010

"Sublimity in Turquoise Blue," *Farrago's Wainscot*, November 2009

"The Indefinite State of Imaginary Morals, Relatives and Gin," *BLIP Magazine*, January 2011

Dedicated to my readers, editors, mentors and friends who have kept me honest. To Richard Peabody for his amazing sense of edge and faith and guidance. To David Everett, Mark Farrington and Tim Wendel for their creative support and to JHU for a place to call my creative home. Especially to my husband, Patrick, and my children, Tyler and Madelyn, and family et al. who have supported and loved the woman, wife, mother, daughter, granddaughter, sister and writer.

Contents

MORE STORIES

Introduction

In this strange world of couplings, women find themselves warily trapped by sex into a reluctant attachment to men; or merely warned by sex of the treachery of connecting.

The tone and style of these stories is oddly addictive; we're listening to the kinds of thoughts no one mentions, thoughts that don't necessarily reflect badly on these women, but do expose a guardedness that seems to be imperative. That guardedness is what we all crawl into at times; here it is the mode of existence.

You know you should be put off by these voices; you know these are women who will never let you in, whether it's friendship or love. On the other hand, you ARE these women sometimes, or you want to be, knowing all too well that dealing with other people's expectations can deplete you; that the ordinary connections are not equal, ever; that there is always more expected from you than you were meant to give, and the best thing to do is to taste what love is like and get out, fast.

Many of her stories start in bed or land in bed, as lovers confront or avoid the demands of love. Does she want to stay? Does she have any need for him? He certainly needs her, and it is this relentlessly intimate need that drives so many of these women away, the rawness, messiness, unattractive infection of love that can cause a woman to gnaw off her arm to sneak away from her sleeping lover.

It's no surprise to find, among these stories, a new Wonder Woman, with a whip. Ah, you say: of course.

—Karen Heuler
Author of *Journey to Bom Goody*
Recipient of the O'Henry Award

The Indefinite State of Imaginary Morals

The Indefinite State of Imaginary Morals, Relatives and Gin

She drinks his Tanqueray and tonic and envisions telling him that he really isn't take-home material or the sort of guy who dresses up 'real well' with all the necessary un-tucking and scarf draping — he's lost too much hair now — though he is satisfactory for a stand-by hook-up — this cannot be denied — or an occasional at-home necking, possibly a low-lighted evening event with coworkers.

Enter gin and tonic #2.

The pillows have pushed out between them. Knees touching. He speaks deep and slow about high school football and stock options. She imagines him tight and angled, ignores the rounded belly. Pictures the thickness of his portfolio instead. She downs the rest of her gin and sucks on the wedge of lime, lets it linger on her lip.

Gin and tonic #3.

Skin to skin. The belly has turned out quite helpful, a fulcrum of sorts, and wouldn't you know it? The belly hides the private parts of their sex so when she glances down to observe the gritty details — really, who can resist? — the mound of flesh will not let her.

Two minutes in, the belly surprises her. It proves to be more flexible than she would have imagined, taking on geometric swing patterns akin to Spyro Gyro, a game she'd so loved as a child, and there in the chaos of belly and breasts, the organs become art, flesh sculptures in motion. She names the penis Waldo and labors to locate its position in the gyrating fleshes between them, like finding the missing character on the back of a cereal box that your little brother waves in the air even though you've told him to Put it down! I'm trying to locate the penis!

It takes the better part of three minutes to find it. The penis works behind a camouflage of gray pubic hair and a love trail. She studies it like Dian Fossey studying apes or a mathematician studying circles and rectangles. She takes measurements by relationships. The arc of the penis equals the slope of the fluted glass. The girth equals the diameter of one in a half sushi rolls. She records the quantitative features, the dedication of it all, for truly, the penis has heart and

4

stick-to-it-ness. A solid ten points for length. Four for width. Bonus points for its dogmatic work ethic. In the end, she awards the penis a handicap for discrepancies between actual breast size and push-up promotional dimensions.

Post-coital water.

Hydration is the single most important step toward anchoring into the reality of sloppy behavior. It is a wetting of the moral palate, a rejuvenation of the spirit, a pause and opportunity to decide if the behavior should register in the grand scheme of lifelong decision makings, or if the behavior is simply a burp, an unanticipated flinch of gastric sluttiness. She finishes the water, wishes it was gin then pulls a pillow into her bare lap. Slutty wins. Yes, it has been a slutty sort of evening.

They are both too worn and wasted and downtime to grab a towel, blanket, napkin, so they sit watching the pieces of spicy salmon with cucumber leftovers on the coffee table, the near-dissipated pools of soy. They talk about the distressed barn wood aesthetic of the room and try to ignore the nakedness of it all and the fact that the room has grown rather cold now and their sweated skins are uncomfortably slippery. Filthy slips. The kind of film one might scrub away with Clorox. When he leans back and offers his shoulder, she nearly cringes like a too old child expected to sit in her grandfather's lap. In minutes, thankfully, he sleeps — it has been so long she's lain still with shallow breath. She hums, in her head, the theme song to *Mission Impossible*, slides from his arm and chest, away from the couch, collects wrinkled clothes from the floor then carries them to the front door where she trips and slips over the skinny black skirt, the red bra that is really too small and the blouse buttons. Shit. She tiptoes back to couch, grabs purse, stops, drops, rolls when he snuffles in his sleep. Crawls back to door.

Coffee.

At the 7-Eleven, around the corner, she stands in a line, waiting to pay for coffee and the Styrofoam cup in her hand. She adjusts the hem of her skinny black skirt and tries to straighten the twist in the red lace bra strap that irritates the mole on her shoulder because the mole sticks out too far. She has made mental notes to have it removed many times. The lace and elastic are cutting into her skin now and she thinks she smells the aroma of ejaculation and sperm swimming through her canal. She glances around the convenience store and wonders if 7-Elevens carry pregnancy tests. The bra strap really is too tight. She sips the lukewarm coffee and laments for the

6

environment and for Styrofoam and the people who made Styrofoam because they didn't know it would be so bad when they invented it. They thought they were saving trees.

What would coffee taste like with Tanqueray? Would it be bitter?

She tells herself, Surely, he will call. How long will it take for him to call? The woman in the security mirror is staring at her now. Her eyes are smudged with mascara and age, framed by a familiar arc in the brows. She used to be so much sexier after sex. The mirror makes her nose convexly large.

Surely, he'll call.

She considers death. It is best served as a pre-emptive measure. She vacillates between great aunt and second cousin and readies the tears because they are more convincing, a quicker getaway. Men run away from women who cry too much. When her cell phone vibrates, she tries to remember which relative she had used last time, not wanting to kill the poor thing twice.

Intolerable Impositions

She gnawed her arm off in the morning,
before he woke. There was no way around it. Her
forearm lay trapped beneath his thick neck
stubbled except for one irritated spot of skin
below the hairline where an infected pore
rounded, tipped with pus. She had seen it the
night before, the infection. She saw it in the dim
bar light, pulsating, but the blemish did not matter
after two glasses of cabernet. And besides, he
presented so well from the front — pressed,
suited, hip-but-not-too-metro tie, square jaw, and
straight white teeth. His hair was thinning.
Inconsequential.

After a tolerable sexing — top, bottom,
behind, sideways, over the edge of the bed — he
turned his back and asked if she would find the
ingrown hair on his neck because it hurt him and
he had no one to do it now that his mother had
passed away three months ago. In the dark silence
of their after-sex, he explained how his mother
cleaned the area with hydrogen peroxide then
extracted the infection, fishing inside with

tweezers and a needle to find the offending hair. He spoke with soft words: "She could always find it so quickly. Now I have no one. Would you mind? The tweezers and the peroxide are in the bathroom cabinet." It was a test, though he did not admit it.

She had known other men like him — men who searched for a dedicated intimate, a partner un-squeamish. It was their way of telling the keepers from the one-nighters. She begged off the immediate task. "I'll do it in the morning," she said, smiling, as if the task did not disgust her.

She woke before him. The bulbous infection lay millimeters from her nose, an inch from her forearm. It would touch her if he rolled backwards, toward her. As long as he lay motionless, she was safe.

Pulling her arm in small increments, she worked it from beneath his neck, but each time her forearm moved, he moved, so that he inched himself backwards, forming into her an intolerable spooning. She had not consented to affections. There was no contract between them for this cuddling, nor was there provision for lovemaking, only sex implied, and she cringed at the familiarity of his back and buttocks and legs where they contacted her skin. It may have been different if he faced her. He was much prettier

9

from the front.

So she rolled to her back, letting only her side and arm touch him now. She considered pulling the arm outright, facing his wakening before leaving a fake phone number. She considered pushing on his right shoulder so to roll him onto his belly, which may have released the arm, but still, it was risky, and would likely wake him that way, too. After endless scenarios imagined — pulling and pushing and facing the man she now loathed for no other reason than the cyst upon his neck — she considered loving him. She could simply stay and wake by his side, share eggs and coffee and *The Washington Post* before returning to bed, but the venture brought the inevitable task of extracting the hair and the pus, and she found herself glaring at the thick, heavy neck with hatred. Only one thing to do.

It took her the better part of an hour to gnaw through the bone. The flesh was easy — soft, pliable, seasoned with skin creams and the experience of her near thirty years. The blood, however, threatened to give her away. It pooled on the mattress beneath them, and he nearly woke from the wet.

As she snuck out of the bedroom, she turned to watch the sleeping man who now clutched her forearm. He pulled it to his chest and hugged it like a child's teddy bear. She remembered mornings when, she too, clutched forearms to her chest. It wasn't so bad. At least they had left her something before leaving.

She tied off the left sleeve of her coat, moved out of the apartment and into the hallway, missing the forearm already but resolved to leaving it. Waking him and his cyst would certainly turn into the day, the week, a year and before long she might consider him more than a fancy. He would fill her life with a series of cystic burdens. He would seize her entirely.

A single forearm was well-worth the escape.

Emperatriz de la Orilla del Río

or

Empress of the Riverbank

She lies on cerulean silk, arms and legs undulating in fleshy waves over bedcovers as if pushing and pulling deep-earth water, a silk and mesquite *cenote* beneath gauze canopy. A breeze washes in from the window. It comes from the river and she imagines the air brings with it the kingfisher's call.

He stands beside the bed, now. Even when he's not there, his smell infects the room — the undershirt he left last Tuesday, the handkerchief she cannot bear to wash. She keeps it on the bedside table, close to her while sleeping and he studies them now, the handkerchief and the woman. He moves to the foot of the bed. Always him moving through the room, behind her closed eyelids during days and nights when she opens herself to other men who never bring her wine or apricots or aberrant poetry, deviant affections. He suspects his infection of her and the weight of his presence in this room.

Mi Emperatriz de la Orilla del Río, he calls her before folding down, tucking himself into her. He whispers in her ear, *Quiero flotar con ti para siempre.* Too soon, he lays pesos on the bedside table, tips his hat.

It is oddly new, the tipping. She tells herself, Certainly, he'll come again tomorrow.

The Empress pulls her back and shoulders and spine curving up from the bed. She crosses wood flooring, opens window shutters. She places bits of raw fish in her hand to entice the bird. On cue, it flies to her, tips its blue featherhead, puffs its orange belly. The Empress imagines the bird puffs in disdain, a proud gesture. They have the same argument every evening.

"You waste yourself on him," the kingfisher says.

"I don't want to hear it."

"A pity."

"I have to eat."

"You will die worn and wasted." The kingfisher picks at a piece of raw fish. "He's left you for good this time. You'll see."

She flicks her hand, sends the kingfisher back

to its river nest.

In her closet hang twenty dresses in increments of color — crimson, saffron, tangerine. She chooses the crimson dress, notices how similar the pattern is to blood drops. She brushes her dark hair, paints her face, readies for the cantina where she will dance with a tray of seven beer bottles on her head, gallivant the floor, spin her dress so the men cannot help but grab at the hem. In time, she will pull pistols from their belts, wave them in the air, watch the men duck beneath her. She will not bring a man home, tonight. She will leave them to their drinking.

They are left.

When she steps free of the dress and stands bare-breasted in the window and moonlight, she breathes in the odors of him left on the handkerchief, in the air. She holds the white cotton close to her neck, listens for the kingfisher's call. She imagines that her day is really the day before playing out in repetition. In thirty years, she'll find herself still a child with this handkerchief close to her neck and shades of him in the room, whispering, *Quiero flotar con vos para siempre.*

Beside the river, she sits, watches the moonlit sheen. An avocado hangs from a nearby branch, dangles over the water. The kingfisher's nest floats nearby, along the riverbank.

"You've left him," the kingfisher says. "I knew you would."

She dips a toe into the cool water, lets her calf, thighs, body fall in, wades to the center where she can no longer touch. She treads so to stay above the surface a moment longer.

"I've left nothing," she says to the bird.

The bird ruffles its feathers, settles down into its water nest as the Empress disappears beneath the halcyon surface. She floats there, between air and another world, close to the kingfisher's nest and the bird studies the water for ripple or bubble, whispers his last words, *Siempre estaras flotando, Emperatriz. Mi amor.*

Fifty Years in Halves

The burrito bowl cilantro-filled and cut by an imaginary line distinguishes her side from his. The big piece of avocado has fallen on his side, hidden behind shredded beef. She rocks it with her fork, as if to say, May I? His eyes are on the pretty girl who has dropped her bottle and stands in a puddle of mango juice and shattered glass.

1st official date + 1 burrito bowl = 2 halves of politeness.

Are you going to eat the avocado bit that has landed on your side of the bowl?

Not if you would like it.

I don't want to impose.

It's yours. He squeezes the soft, green piece between fingertips, moves it to her mouth. She opens lips, uses her tongue to accept the

16

smush. The offer turns to promise and sex, maybe another date. He wipes his fingers clean.

She chews, eyes on table.

Would you like to see a movie this weekend? he says.

1 month + 1 burrito bowl = 1 whole of familiarity.

She sees the avocado bit that sits closest to him, barely over the half line. She plays with it, bored. They've been to this restaurant four times in four weeks and it has grown familiar. She pokes it with her fork; he sees her playing, says nothing. She sees that he sees, kisses him for his silent acquiescence.

1 year + 1 burrito bowl = 2 halves of irritability.

You don't like avocado much, do you? she says, eyeing his side of the bowl.

I never said that.

But you always let me have it.

You assume.

She forks the avocado. He turns away to watch the corrugated metal wall, where he sees her in striped versions, dull and shiny, stealing the avocado. She turns to watch a handsome man, who notices the couple turned away from each other.

1st date + 18 years of children, soccer carpools, workaday commutes + 1 burrito bowl = 2 halves of misunderstood apathy.

The avocado flesh is bigger now, covered in cilantro, swollen like diapers, carpools, a promise about abortions and other secrets. Steam rises. She remembers nights of wanting him, nights of being wanted and angry for the nights he turned away. She forks the flesh, stabs prongs so completely that metal tips scrape at acrylic-covered table top. She pops the flesh into her mouth because it is more dismissive to pop than to slide or simply move. She chews and stares at his fat, thick, balding head.

Fifty years of dates + 1 burrito bowl = 1 whole of understanding.

He is covert now. Tips the avocado toward his side of the bowl then turns down his hearing aid to miss the inevitable treatise on why she should have it. He takes her hand, squeezes it gently and watches her lips move, remembering their first burrito bowl and how she stole his avocado, how she was so jealous when he looked at a pretty girl with mango-soaked shoes. He smiles, lifts himself on feeble legs, kisses her withered cheek. Pinching the avocado with shaking fingertips, he lays it on her tongue.

Featherbedding

He brings her water and miniature corn
muffins, halved open and spread with bright
green pepper jelly. They are from a glass jar she's
kept all these years. She lengthens bare legs down
the mattress, sets the four muffin halves side by
side on the white cloth napkin he's unfolded for
her, lain over her thighs like a tablecloth.

She's not eaten today. This is the last of their
food.

Nothing left in the cabinet or refrigerator or
the hiding places neither of them tells each other
about. The muffins are necessary now, like the
moment when a child knows there are no magical
gift givers or tooth fairies or St. Christophers.
Only mortals and starvation.

Something pitiful in the way he holds them, as
if an offering.

She sets the muffins aside, opens herself,
nymph-like, mouth spread and gritty. She pulls
the dirty edge of his gray t-shirt up so to show
herself to him, spreads herself across the mattress
like thin flesh oil over too much canvas. He
moves over her, pushes her thicker sections,

spreads her more thinly, more evenly so to smooth out the bruises and lines. He can see through her now, understand her better. He falls in love with her anyway.

He calls her Calliope and sings a song for her about swimming in a stream, the deep part where they twine thin hungry legs, tread water, pull back their heads and fall beneath the surface so to kiss long water kisses. They ignore the bruises.

Fill me, my darling
Pour yourself.

He digs a trench for her, forms a mote around her body, rips mattress and blanket and sheets and feather pillows to better pad the nest. He says: we can wait out the winter here in feathers and mattress springs. Then he burrows beneath her, turns his body, settles beneath her.

I want you on top of me forever.

But we haven't any food. We'll waste away.

She lays flat against him, warms her breasts and stomach, pushes her legs and arms against his. Where their skins touch, they grow moist and warm and he imagines they could grow sustenance, a garden between their skins. He tries to pull feathers up and onto her back so to warm her, but they've floated off the bed and onto the floor. They stay this way for days.

Where are the muffins? she says.

They sit stale now, on the bedside table, feathers caked in the hardened green pepper jelly.

Pity, she says, my mother had given it to me. The jelly, I mean. She falls out over him. Should have eaten it while it was still fresh.

Stage Play in Five Acts of Her: Matinee

DRAMATIS PERSONÆ
She — Is a puppet.
I — Live inside her except when she lets me out to play.
We — Are always together.
He — Will be mentioned only once.

ACT ONE

She stands on hardwood. Long porcelain arms covered in three-quarter sleeves hide near-faded bruises. Her mouth forms a perfect O framed with red clown lips. She learned the O from years of practice. Practice, he called it. She sings the vowel, pushing it from diaphragm and out through the theatre. She ignores the hands beneath her.

Stagehands watch her from the trapdoor now. They fondle and move her. Their fingernails are dirt-caked and sharp and she ignores them, calls to her audience of one who sits in a red velvet seat. Cue me.

It is ironic, her watching me watching her, because we are the same, and I might cry for her if sentimentality had been a strength. I watch her jostle and feel nothing.

Ignore them, she says. It is her only line in this act and it is unnecessary.

She bends at waist so to push forward and spread herself deliberately, balancing and throwing out arms and hands curved like a porcelain doll's, palms stretched, growing like tentacles over red velvet seatbacks. Like drifting seaweed, her fingers beckon. They pluck me from my seat, pull me, glide me to stage, where she stands me at her hip, denying me the space inside her head and I try not to look at it, the space inside her head, because I do not want her to think I want it.

ACT TWO

We swoon under hot lights melting the wax of our face. We can smell the face wax. It melts like candy paraffin filled with pastel pink and green and yellow sweet sugar syrup glistening with the dew from our mouths. We cannot smile. The makeup will not let us. Our mouth is an infinite O and our eyes pierce through baked on mascara.

We are hollowed out and old and used, cracked from stage lights, but between the cracking, beneath the grime, we are perfect. It does not matter. No one will want us soon. We are a dying art.

ACT THREE

Say it. Say it out loud. Sing it to the world. Let me inside so I can help you. I point. There, look, you have an audience. The velvet seats fill with people she always knew but not really. She has hidden herself behind brocade and red clown lips for many years.

There is your mother. I point. Your father. I point again. Your brother, sister, cousin, second cousin, and your aunt who we all believed to be an alien clone. I go on, pointing out all the patrons who might listen. But she stands, mouth still, a maiden caught in stage lights.

Coward.

She tries to cry but her makeup will not let her form the face and so the tears fall in two thin lines between nose and cheeks, along her big wide O.

ACT FOUR

I could have written her as is with long bushy hair, skinned knees, overhauls, blueberry stains on her fingers and teeth because she eats them too much. I love her better this way, blueberry-stained and wild.

I shuffle dance close to her, in front of her, to the side. I move to make her laugh, break the freeze. When I trip on purpose, she laughs accidently in a short burst of air. Her arms fall to her side then wrap at her waist like they used to when she ate blueberries and laughed accidentally out loud and finally, I think, she will shed the brocade, crack the face, but as I watch and wait, her arms form again, stretching out in curves. She bends at waist. Feet spread over the trapdoor. The stagehands jostle her.

ACT FIVE

Do you remember when I slipped in the snow and you stood laughing? I was not so mad about the groceries, and I did not hate you so much then, because I still loved you like déjà vus. I loved you so much that I wrote you into this play. Remember?

She does not move or wrap her arms, does not accidentally laugh or sigh. She says: You can come in. And she pulls at her ear and opens her head like a hinged trapdoor.

No. I want you to come out.

ACT SIX: The unplanned act like one last try. A last call before closing.

Remember the time you laughed three times? The snow was nothing, a trifle, but you laughed because it was funny and then you laughed when we broke our ankle — I stop because I realize I've spoken of us again, we as in a collective.

Yes, it was funny, she says. He.... She stops short because he was only supposed to be mentioned once, a second mentioning was not in the script, and now I've added a third. She corrects herself. The person who will not be named stood in front of the train, between us and the train as it kept coming. That person did not move until we were safe.

That person broke our ankle pulling us to safety. That person broke other things, too.

We stop because the sentiment is like filling a shot glass at last call. Half full, half empty, clock ticking.

We jostle again, wince, crack our makeup a little more. A broken marionette with no strings. We hold still, wait for the stagehands to remove their fingers and drag us, brocade heels over hardwood, to our place behind the red velvet curtain, where we will wait for the evening show to begin. All the best people will come to see us.

Cystic Burden

Comedone tipped with ethic, seeping ipseity.

Monk Man and Moonshine

*We are here and it is now. Further than
that, all human knowledge is moonshine.*

— *Henry Louis Mencken*

"When the Devil knocks on your door, you
just say get thee behind me Satan." Grandma
Sylkie flicked the cigarette between her index and
middle fingers, her greatest talent. The ashes
disappeared into a water-spotted, blue-green
ceramic bowl sitting squat on the arm's length
Rubbermaid table covered in blue, pink and white
flowers, a plastic tablecloth cut to measure.

The girl watched her grandmother's face, her
earnest, gentle eyes, red-rimmed from early
morning canning, cabbages and onions. At five
years of age, the eyes had been everything. At
thirteen, the eyes hollowed into etched skin. They
pooled worry and loss for a run-off daughter,
drowned son, a workaday husband more grease
and car parts than lover. The girl reveled that she

29

knew what a lover was — low gruff noises late at night. The old woman's lines shifted with another drag of her cigarette. The lines formed into puckered lips and squinted eyes and the old woman aged in the seconds the girl studied her. *Yes, this is my future.*

"Has the Devil ever visited you, grandma?"

"A time or two, but I've never kept his company for long. Your Mama, that's another story."

The girl bent her head to the weathered, green turf stretched over concrete, worn through in a narrow path from stairs to screen door, frayed bare in sections.

"Don't worry, possum. The devil ain't none to be scared of. You'll know him when you see him." Grandma Sylkie took another drag. "It's the Monk Man you ought to worry about. The Monk'll get you in the night without so much as knocking." She held the cigarette with long ash tip out to the side then leant in on her chair as if telling a secret. "If he ever comes for you, just holler nice and loud. Me and Grandpa'll be there." Her eyes took a gentler slope again and she put her hand out, rested it on the girl's knee. "Go get your shoes on now. Grandpa'll be ready to go 'fore long."

The blue canvas sneakers had rips in the toes that let too much dirt in, but dried fast. Good for creeking. She took a Debbie Snack from the clear jar with the tin lid and threw the plastic wrapper on the porcelain counter that had worn through at the corners and edges, dark metal through white. None of her friends' parents had countertops like this. None of her friends lived with their grandparents. She joined Grandma Sylkie again on the porch where she ate the long peanut butter and cookie and chocolate cakes.

"Promise you'll watch out for the moccasins."

"We don't have water moccasins, Grandma. I learned in school —"

"Don't you tell me what we have and don't have. I seen 'em. You just try to step clear and don't —"

Look them in the eyes. The girl's mind formed sarcasm like Sunday morning boredom and though she said the words silently, the old woman saw them in her. The old woman could private words like coming rain and tornadoes.

The girl quickly changed her words. *The Lord is my shepherd, I shall not want. He maketh me to lie down in green pastures....*

"Watch your sass girl. More than one sass been caught by the charmer. Mind me, else it'll charm you too."

The girl nodded. Yes, she knew the story well.

Grandpa Ernie made his way from the garage. His blue overalls and work boots covered in engine grease. He smiled when he saw the girl ready and waiting on the porch. When he stepped

31

up, tall and straight, the girl waited for him to kneel down so she could wrap her arms around his neck, smell the old cars and dirt and engine grease on his skin and in his gray hair. She would remember the smells of him as a woman and dream them on a grassy hilltop.

"Grab us a couple of RCs."

The girl ran to the garage where the soda cooler sat in the corner. He'd bought the cooler from Mr. Henry when the diner shut down. The cooler now stood, covered in grease too.

"You're gonna rot her teeth out, Ernie."

"No worse than those Debbie Snacks you buy her."

"You won't let her wander off this time? You're gonna watch her close?"

"Yeah, I'll watch her."

"She's too young to go romping up in those woods."

"My granddaddy had me up in those woods younger than she is now."

"I'm just scared —"

"I said I'd watch her, Sylk." He sat and lit a cigarette. "Besides, she's not likely to go wandering with all those stories you put in her head. She's not right for it."

"Better she knows. Thirteen."

"Ain't nothin' to know, Sylk. Tales is all. Scaring her more by telling them." He paused long enough to consider his next words though they were inevitable. She had to hear them.

"Didn't do much good for Jenny or Jacob — "

"Don't talk 'bout the dead to me old man." She gazed across the small lawn to the road between the house and line of cypress trees bordering the creek. She couldn't see the creek from the porch. She didn't need to see it. It was there just as it always been. "Just watch her."

"Said I'd watch her."

The sun had almost touched the Appalachian ridge as they left Marietta and crossed the river into West Virginia, emptying their RC bottles. Grandpa started humming one of his favorites he played on an eight track by the leather recliner. His voice sounded of hills and skipping stones.

"What're we doing there tonight, Grandpa?"

"The still's been kicking off again. I told Grandma Freid I'd take a look at it." He stretched his neck left and winced. "Why one of them boys can't do it, I don't know. Lazy, whole lot of 'em."

They turned down a dirt road nearly hidden in the break of trees. It lay beneath Great Grandma Freid's white house perched high up on the hill. Sarah turned from the great white house, caught a glimpse of the single pump at the tree line. The small pump moved up and down at a steady pace.

Grandpa Ernie parked the truck into a rattled and stop. "Grab the flashlights." He pointed to the glove box.

The sky stretched in periwinkle and fireflies and honeysuckle air. The old man led the way down a narrow dirt path.

"Darn it!" The girl stomped her foot.

The old man smiled.

"Forgot my jar."

"We'll find you t'nother up at the hooch." He held out his hand and the girl took it, swinging their hands between them as they walked. He raised his arm up high, as he often did, and she pirouetted beneath it. He kept his arm raised in case she wanted to turn again but she stopped at one then took a breath.

"Grandpa?"

"Yeah."

"Have you ever seen the Monk Man?"

"Can't say I have."

"Grandma Sylk says I should watch out for him."

"Then I 'spect you should."

"She says he'll snatch me in my sleep if I'm not careful."

The old man winced at this. He walked, slowed now, and after a time he spoke in low whispers though they were in the trees and he could have yodeled with no one to hear him.

"I shouldn't be telling you this, being you're young and all but since your Grandma went and told you 'bout him, I suppose I should tell you the rest."

"The rest?"

"How to make him go 'way in case he ever shows up." The old man shone his flashlight at either side of the path, until the light casted upon a honeysuckle bush. The bush grew close to an old oak. Vines wrapped up and around the ancient trunk. "Come here. Hold out your hand."

He picked three honeysuckle blooms and laid them side by side on the girl's palm then shone the flashlight on them. The pink-red hue of the girl's skin gave the yellow blooms a rosy backdrop and they appeared exotic or heavenly, pieces of a fairytale in light circles. "If that Monk Man ever comes for you, just drink one of these."

"Honeysuckle?"

"This ain't no simple honeysuckle, child. This vine grows close by an oak, up from the same earth and roots. Oaks are special, all of them. God's trees. These blooms," he pointed to the tiny yellow flowers in her hand. "They'll keep you safe."

"But there's only three. What if he comes for me more than three times?"

The old man smiled. She was a smart girl, always figuring ahead.

"Then we should pick more so you can keep them by the bedside."

"What about winter?"

He cinched his brows in tight. "Guess we

could always pick a mess then make wine. Keep it in a jar by the bed for the winter."

"Really, Grandpa? We can make honeysuckle wine? Will it work?"

"Sure it will. We'll make some this fall 'fore it gets cold. Enough to keep till summer."

The girl grabbed the old man around the waist, squeezed tight.

"All right. Let's get going. It'll be pitch dark."

Along the path a soft creaking noise joined in with the cricket's song and the old man picked up his pace. He did not take the girl's hand. He did not need to.

The wooden shack stood with snake and raccoon skins dangled from rusty nails. The girl had watched the old man and kin skin many of the animals—squirrels, coons, rabbit. The skins were home and self-preservation. But the lock hanged loose, broken.

"Stand here by this tree. Don't move."

She did as told, watched the old man take hold of the door pulling it wide. Before disappearing into the shack, he turned to her. "I mean it, stay right there."

She nodded into the beam of light.

Critter sounds scuffled and flapped — an owl hoot, a crack of branch, dried leaves scattering. Sounds of goodness. It was the quiet that called for worry.

Fireflies lit within inches of each other now and the girl put her honeysuckle blooms carefully in her jeans pocket then took a Mason jar sitting against the hooch. She tip-toed round back, stopping every few steps like a statue in a sculpture game she played at Bible School. A glow lighted in a slow fade pattern. She held her palms close together, not quite touching and in one quick movement, she surrounded the firefly. Its wings flitted against her fingers and palms and she peeked between her thumbs to watch it glow, remembering a silly rhyme Billy Barnhart had told her after Sunday School four weeks ago when she agreed to walk down by the creek with him. He spoke in rhymes and grinned — *this is the church, this is the steeple.* He grabbed her chest and she punched him in the nose then was sad for punching him and wondered if he might grab her again. The firefly fluttered against her palms, rested at one side, worn out and glowing in slow pulses.

"What'cha doin' out here by your lonesome?"

She jumped at the voice. The firefly flew out of her hands. With an irritated glance, she turned to the boy-man's dark silhouette against a tree. He held his Daddy's shotgun sideways in his hands. Forever he held that gun like a talisman.

"You scared me, Randy Freid!"

"Probably not as much as you scared that

firefly." He moved closer, playfully. "You're out here all alone?"

"No." Her right toe turned in. "Grandpa's checking the still."

"I told Grandma Freid I'd do that."

"Guess Grandpa beat you to it. He says you're lazy."

The boy-man shook his head then started toward the front, calling Sarah after him. "Come on. Shouldn't be round here in the dark like that. Might get bit." He pinched at her side.

She giggled.

Grandpa Ernie came out of the shack, a mixture of purrs and sputters behind him. "Did you do this?" He pointed to the broken lock.

Randy shifted nervously on his feet. "Forgot the key. I planned on fixing it."

"Mm, hm. Think I know what's wrong with it."

"I was goin' to fix that too."

"Didn't you say that two nights ago?"

The boy-man hung his head.

"It's runnin' now but it needs a few parts. I can get them tomorrow in town and bring them out —"

"I can get them."

"Know what you need? S'pose you could come on in with us tonight. Grandma Sylk'll have some dinner waiting. I can show you what you need tomorrow. Save me a trip."

"Yeah, all right."

The boy-man followed in his daddy's old sun-worn Chevy that was more rust than red. At the house, fried catfish waited, boiled corn on the cob. Grandma Sylk put a glass of milk on the table and two empty glasses for the men. The old man grabbed a jar of moonshine from the cupboard.

"Might as well try the new batch."

Randy grinned and Grandma Sylk shook her head. The old man poured the two glasses half full. The girl watched as they drank.

Randy winked at her. "Wanna taste?"

"No, she don't." Grandma Sylk gave him the stink eye.

"One little sip won't hurt her."

The girl glanced at the old man who sat silent, watching them. He smiled

"Well, I guess a sip won't hurt her."

Grandma Sylk huffed but everyone ignored her. The girl took the glass in both hands and tipped it to her lips. By increments she lifted the glass bottom until the moonshine wetted her tongue. When a few more drops of it poured into her mouth, she pushed the glass away and swallowed the little bit then breathed in a fresh wave of air, pushed the coolness in and out, tried to douse the fire on her tongue. She coughed.

"Good lesson for you." Grandma Sylk sounded pleased.

Randy clapped his cousin on the back. "You'll get used to it before long."

"No, she won't."

The old man watched the girl with pride. "Reckon it's time for bed."

The hand tasted of sweat and moonshine and Marlboro cigarettes.

The girl pushed it away. "You scared the life out of me!"

"Quiet. If you wake Grandpa and Grandma and I'll not be able to take you with me."

"Take me where?"

"To the field."

"Why would I wanna go tromping through some field in the middle of the night with you?"

"Trust me. You want to go." He collected the Mason jar from the bedside table and waved it in the air. "Get dressed quick, and meet me outside, but be quiet. If you wake them, they'll make you go back to bed." The boy-man left the room, carrying the Mason jar with him.

They walked behind the house where it was darkest, but for the big moon. When they'd crested the ridge, he pointed below and the girl caught her breath.

"It's like Christmas in summer," she said.

"I thought you'd like it."

The girl imagined fairies spreading pollen and daisies and the bleeding hearts Grandma loved so much.

He started down the hill. "Come on."

She ran after him. They chased fireflies, scooped handfuls from the air, pushed them into the Mason jar. In minutes, they lay exhausted, side by side on the grassy rise. The moon, nearly full, shone bright, dulling the stars that framed it. He sat up and pulled a flask full of moonshine from his back pocket.

"Want some?"

He handed the silver flask to her. She sipped and coughed, sipped some more. She transformed herself older.

"Careful." He pulled the flask from her, smiled when she tried to take it back. They lay on the ground, the Mason jar above her, sideways against the sky. Iridescent wings and glowing tails.

"Thanks."

"You're welcome."

"Are you going to fix the still?"

"Yeah. Tomorrow. Grandpa Ernie's going to help me."

"Have you heard anything from your Mama?" This stopped them both. She made herself not turn to him, watch his discomfort.

He put a hand on her arm and with his other hand took the jar from her, considered it, sat it on the ground beside him as if taking a toy from a child. *No you've played with it long enough.* "I knew you'd like it out here. No one else, at least no one my age seems to slow down long enough to care about things like this." He sat up and drank from the flask. When he turned to her, the girl acted as though she didn't notice him. "Mama liked nights like this. She used to bring me out here." He turned away from her.

She put a hand on his back.

"Thanks for coming out here," he said then moved closer so that the girl could smell his breath.

"Can I ask you a question?"

"What kind of question?"

"It's a good question but I don't know if you'll want to answer."

"How will I know unless you ask it?"

"Okay, I'll ask it then. Have you ever been kissed?"

It was the question she might have expected if she had let herself or even the question she would have wanted. "Not really," she said.

She welcomed them. Forehead, mouth, the taste of cigarettes in his mouth because it was so different than the peanut butter and jelly sandwiches that Billy Barnhart's mother made for him.

He pulled away. "I shouldn't have done that."

"We should go back."

He pulled the flask out again, tipped it up, jiggled it a little. Nothing.

"We should go back," she repeated.

"You won't tell..."

"I won't tell." She stood until he grabbed her arm, pulled her back down.

"I didn't mean to...." The grip was tight, skin against bone.

"I want to go home."

"Just give me a minute. I need to think." When he didn't let go on the third and fourth, she pulled back, out of his hand, jumped up and made her way to the top of the ridge. He followed.

"Damn it, Sarah!" He struggled up the hillside, fell to his knees, punched at the ground. "Sarah, stop! Come back!"

She'd left the Mason jar full of fireflies. The Honeysuckle, she had left by the bedside.

She ran into a grouping of trees and hid behind a thick trunk, nearly missed the honeysuckle vine that grew up and around it, straight out of the ground as if it had no roots of its own but shared its roots with the tree and she repeated this, shared roots with the tree just like Grandpa Ernie. The vine climbed high up into the canopy twisted around the lower branches. Was it an oak? She didn't need to see it with her eyes. It must be an oak. God had put it there for her.

"Where are you?" Randy sang out, now playfully, laughing, apologizing in a way that could

43

mean things. His mama had been a mean drunk.

With shaking fingers, she grabbed a tiny bloom, pulling it from the vine. She pinched the end with her a thumb and index nail, severing it, pulled the stamen back and let the dew fall.

"I see you," Randy sang out, closer now.

When his hands took hold, she screamed and it startled them both. They fell to the ground, Randy on top.

"Get off of me!" She kicked. He struggled to grab hold.

"Stop it, Sarah. Just a minute. I'm not going to hurt —"

When the shotgun muzzle appeared at his chin, the girl and the boy-man fell still.

"Boy, you better stand up 'fore I blow your head clean off."

Grandpa Ernie cracked the muzzle against Randy's jaw, cutting it. Blood ran down his neck. When he cursed, Grandpa Ernie cracked him hard over the head. He fell sideways to the ground.

"Come on, Sarah. Let's get you home." Grandpa Ernie pulled her up and to his side. They left Randy on the ground and said nothing as they made their way home. Sarah held her arms about her waist and chest.

Grandma Sylk wasn't on the porch. She waited in her brown leather recliner, up straight. She sipped black coffee from a china cup. A smoking cigarette lay in the glass ashtray. When she saw the girl's disheveled hair, full of twigs and dirt, she cried out and took the child into her arms and the girl cried, too, suddenly aware of the weight of it all and Randy still in the field, the Mason jar with fireflies. She began to mutter clipped phrases and words: "We didn't do anything... the flask... fireflies in the jar... it wasn't his fault." She didn't notice the silent glances shared between the old man and woman. "I'm sorry, I'm so sorry."

The door slammed behind Grandpa Ernie as he headed back outside with the shotgun.

"Is he going to shoot him? He's going to shoot him isn't he and he'll die and it'll all be my fault."

"S'pect he might."

"I'm sorry. I'm so sorry." The girl cried.

"You're not the first to do it. We've all followed the Monk a time or other. At least, now, you know what he looks like."

When Grandpa Ernie brought Randy back, he made him sit on the porch while Grandma called his daddy. The next hours flew with curses and crying from the porch, through the screen door like fire and steam left off a pressure cooker. The men yelled about old debts and forgotten birthdays and "Randy would never do that" and "I saw him do it." Randy's daddy used the word whore, "no better than her Mama." Grandpa

Ernie told him to leave and to take his heathen boy with him. He told them to never come back.

Sarah pulled the afghan over her shoulders. The air was cool but sometimes the porch was the best place to breathe. Fireflies floated over the small front lawn, between the porch and the garage and the old man and woman and the girl watched them. Time to time, the girl's eyes drifted off to the line of trees at the road.

"Do you miss him, Grandma?" she said.

"Who, possum?"

"Jacob."

The old woman's voice changed. "Yes, I do."

"Do you think it hurt when he drowned?"

"Don't know."

"I think it did."

Grandma Sylkie's eyes watered up. "Why would you say that?"

"Randy's drowning, too, I think."

"I told you not to say his name anymore. We're not going to speak of him."

"He didn't do anything wrong. Not really. It was as much me as him."

The old woman stood, walked to the girl and slapped her hard across the cheek. "Don't you ever say a thing like that again. We'll not speak of it anymore. You hear?"

The girl wiped the tears off her cheeks.

"Honeysuckle doesn't keep the Monk Man away, does it?"

Grandpa Ernie bent his head.

"They're all different," the old woman said. "The Monks, they all have their ways. Never know what will stop them. Best not to be chasing fireflies and moonshine in the middle of the night though."

"Is that what Mama did? Chase fireflies and moonshine?"

The old woman quieted and lit another cigarette. "Your mama chased a lot of things."

"Like Jacob? She said she wanted to chase him right into the river and drown with him. She said that was why she couldn't take care of me, because she'd already drown with him and I would, too, if I stayed with her."

Grandpa Ernie stood and headed out to the garage, walking through the lazy fireflies. Sarah watched them dance around him.

"Grandma? Do you think fireflies are happy in a jar?"

The old woman flicked her cigarette.

"I don't think they like it much. I think they'd rather be floating around." Sarah stood. "Maybe Mama wanted to float too like Jacob." The girl didn't look at her grandmother as she headed toward the front door. "I'm going to bed."

She washed her face and brushed her teeth, put on the soft pink flannels the old woman had left on top of the quilt. When she crawled into bed, tucking her feet beneath the star-patterns, she let the warmth of the bed build until it spread from her toes into her legs. She snuggled into the sensation, making sure to cup her hand so not to crush the three shriveled honeysuckles that lay there in her palm. She spread her fingers and gazed at the blooms then she lay them each on the bedside table, one at a time, just in case.

Sublimity in Turquoise Blue

"Swim."

Saltwater, turquoise blue, climbs into alpine waves, inchoate. White foam crests at the tips, reach to the sky as if the foam might lift off and float.

It could happen — saltwater clouds. It could happen in a poem on a canvas, a symphony. Saltwater clouds are a metaphorical possibility for an artist, for a painter, but I'm not an artist today, nor am I a painter. Today, I'm drowning in Mexico.

Survival for Artists 101

When faced with near-death experiences, artists tend to take pause. Artists are no good at survival. They see pain as swatches of experience, and the mere act of survival is too precious to ignore in lieu of life. To the artist, sublimity is a rare gift, so it is one not to be wasted. For this reason, never leave an artist alone gazing into the face of death. The artist will likely fall in love.

"Swim! You have to swim!" Peter is at least five yards away, and I'm still watching the turquoise wave as it forms before me. So tall, so beautiful.

"I can't." It's all I can manage out of fear and beauty, and Peter cannot hear me; he has disappeared behind another wave. The churning water twists my arms and legs, and I kick wearily. "I can't."

I can't fully taste the saltwater on my lips or feel the drops of saltwater trickling down into my lungs. I can't fully sense these things. I know they are there, but I can't experience them as they're meant to be experienced, because the turquoise water is coiling higher onto itself, arching over me, and my breath is shallow. I'm caught in the depths, in the *salvage azul*. The ocean is more powerful than I'll ever be.

Survival for Artists: Drowning

A shock must be administered to pull an artist out of herself. Even threat of death is not enough. One must ruffle the most primal and inward sensibilities in order to break through an experience of sublimity. One must *Snap!* the artist out, so to speak. Using the ego is most often the best way. Even in the face of sublimity, an artist can always feel her need to be better than what she is.

Sublimity gives way to terror when I turn toward the beach, the narrow expanse of dry, safe sand. There I see the beachcombers and walkers now taking pause in their strolls to watch the two tourists caught in the waves. What must they be thinking? It can't be good. They just stand there, watching.

Foolish. Yes, I feel foolish.

A creeping, vulnerability pulses at the back of my skull, erupting in tiny fissures: fear, excitement, lack of oxygen, humility, embarrassment, the kids, God, the kids.

God? Agnostic atrophy.

Time spreads seconds into slow chronologies of one instant after another — kick, breathe, kick, breathe — and a drop of white foam falls down ricocheting off the water's surface. It lands in my eye. Saltwater in the eye. Salt water tears. No, not tears, just one tear. No need to be dramatic.

But there are so many drops — water, water everywhere — but this is a story about water, not water itself, and so one drop will do.

Saltwater tears are for the crocodiles, and they don't swim in the ocean. Crocodiles swim in the lagoon on the other side of the peninsula, I think, and I'm full of adrenaline now, not tears. Tears are for after, so it is a false tear that has landed in my eye. Just one. One before the wave crashes down.

Turning toward shore, the wave grows behind me. I don't see it, but I know it's there. I'm watching the rocks. They mock me; the flat rocks that all but hide in the sand, lining the edge between surf and beach. They know. They know they're the only reason I can't let the waves roll me into shore. They know.

I saw them before, the rocks. I felt them, too. They felt like foreboding.

"Foreboding how?" my professor would say.

"Foreboding what," I answer. "Death warnings."

Survival for Artists: Collecting Resonance

Details. Always the details. An artist should never let details go unnoticed. Painting the right details will resonate with the observer one hundred years from now.

"Think before you swim," the rocks said to me forebodingly. I heard their warnings, and I had even thought to pause, but I'm always pausing, always thinking. For once, I wanted to swim first, think later. And so I did. I swam first, think later, thought later, will think, will have thought.

I'm thinking now.

52

The rocks seem so far away now that I'm in the water, but one strong wave, one wrong break. . . . I push the thought away.

It's much easier to recognize danger when in the moment, but so much easier to consider the danger thereafter.

Breathe. The turquoise coil falls, breathe, and I dive beneath the foam. The wave pulls, beating against my back, churning my arms and legs. Air, I need air, but the wave churns, and it won't let me surface.

How far behind is the next one? They're coming much faster now. From shore, they had seemed so graceful.

My chest hurts.

Survival for Artists: Hallucinations

Let hallucinations take the artist where they may. Life, death, whatever the outcome, at least the surreal will offer something more than the humdrum experience. The upshot is, if the artist survives, she will have something much more interesting to share.

Stay beneath the water, the voice says. It's my voice, I know this, but it's the only voice speaking, and so it would be rude to ignore it. *Stay here, beneath the water, where it's safe.* I can feel the beginning of the next wave pulling, and so I swim

53

to the bottom and stay. I stay and open my eyes.

The saltwater stings, but I keep them open anyway. The water pushes, and I push back, letting air bubble out of my nose.

The tide pulls me to where the water is deeper, gentler, but my lungs won't hold forever; I know this, but there's no negotiating with water and waves.

My chest hurts.

Survival for Artists: Emotion

When the artist is angry and unable to change or control the situation, it is best for the artist to blame the offending situation on someone else. It will not change the outcome of the situation, but it will help to funnel the artist's emotion. Family and friends are good for these purposes. They offer the most opportunity for practice in times of minor stress, so when trauma hits, the artist will be prepared.

"Come on, the water's fine." I can still see Peter's frame against the approaching waves, calling me out. It's all his fault, and now I'm in this damnable ocean beneath the waves.

Just off in the distance, beneath the water, I see two figures playing and laughing on the ocean floor, just as they were on the beach before I swam out.

Two figures — boy and girl. They are playing in the sand, and I know who they are, even before I can see their faces, hidden beneath blue and pink sombreros. They are as familiar to me as my own skin. Giggles erupt from under the wide hats.

We had purchased them, the sombreros not the children, at the Mayan market, along the dirt road that led us to Chichén Itzá. The Mayans stood in front of the market passing out free shots of tequila.

The hats were so big that we couldn't help but laugh. "Look, Mommy." My daughter grabbed her hips and clapped her feet on the floor. The Mayans had laughed with us.

"Look, Mommy." My daughter's voice is now muted beneath the water. She eyes me with big brown eyes and sunburned cheeks then points to the hole she's made in the ocean floor. A perimeter of little red flags stands guard around it.

"The flags mean that you shouldn't go in there. The water is too rough." My son was always the practical one.

I reach out to them, my daughter and son, a gesture I've repeated so many times over the years, a stroke to their cheeks, their hair. A quick, gentle gesture that always meant there would be more of them. Never had I touched their cheeks believing it to be the last.

Certainly, this is the last. Just one more touch.

In a flash of light they disappear, and in their

places appear litters of laughing resort tourists reclining on plastic chaises holding margaritas and bottled waters in their hands. One man holds up a tiny plastic pyramid.

"I came to Mexico, and all I got was this plastic Mayan temple." He thinks he's funny.

He hands me the temple. The inscription reads, "Chichén Itzá." I have one back in the hotel room, but I don't tell him this. I would never have bought it if not for my daughter's batting eyelashes. These things help me sleep at night: "I'd never have done it if it weren't for the children's eyelashes."

"What would the ancient Mayans think?" I say more to myself then the man, but he answers me anyway.

"They're dead, you know." He looks at me the way a conservative looks at a liberal, and I look back at him, a liberal watching a conservative. "You know they're dead, right? These new Mayans, they aren't the ancient ones."

I might have said something spiteful, certainly sarcastic, but I'm drowning, and so I nod. I'm not proud of it, but sometimes placation is the mother of survival, and if it works . . .

The man seems to dismiss the tension between us and looks at the plastic pyramid in his hand. "I bought this one off'a one of those contemporary Mayans at the Chicken Itza walkway. You know, outside the watering hole.

They wouldn't sell them if they minded."

I almost correct his 'chicken,' but it would be a waste of air. Besides, he said it just to rouse me. I can see it in the narrow of his eyes. The man sips his margarita then disappears into the blue water.

In his place appears Rafael, the Chichén Itzá tour guide. Rafael reclines, grinning on his chaise lounge. He's holding a bottle of water.

"What're you doing here?" I ask with an emphasis on you.

"I'm a guide aren't I?" He holds up the bottle. "Gringos can't handle the Mexican water. Our water is too rich with . . ." He pauses for the right word. "Minerals? Yes, the minerals. Our water is too rich with the minerals. Our water flows through the caves, through the Earth. Earth water, like blood."

I nod in understanding, but water knowledge has little consequence when a person is drowning.

"But why are you here?" Emphasis on here.

"I'm your tour guide."

"But I'm drowning."

"Yes, I know." He smiles.

"I need a lifeguard."

"You're in Mexico, Señora. There are no life guarders here. In Mexico, you have to guard your own. Didn't you see the flags?"

I would have offered the obligatory sigh, out of frustration, but being under the water and all.

"I can't help you. I'm not real." Rafael shrugs then stands. "But I can guide you through your drowning." He smiles and turns to face the Mayan temple now rising from the ocean floor. There are red flags all around it. Rafael points to them. "The flags, they're there for a reason."

"Yes." In my youth, I'd have rolled my eyes, but through the years, I've learned to take my lessons with more grace.

Rafael gives me a fatherly glance then leads me to the temple. We walk hand in hand. "The temple isn't particularly big," he says, "not like the sun temple, but it's tall."

Not tall enough to crest the water's surface, of course. Irony and all.

"Kulkulkan," Rafael points to the long stone serpents that border either side of the temple steps. "The feathered serpent god." Both mouths gape open with fangs and rolling, distended tongues. "The temple faces the sun's path." Rafael points up to the surface where the turquoise blue waves still roll. "The Mayans followed the sun and the moon."

"What is the serpent for?"

"A reminder that life renews."

"But I don't want to renew. I want to live. I want to live this life, now."

He smiles and points to the red flags again.

"I want to go home."

"You can't go home yet, señora. You're on

58

vacation." With a wave of his hand, the temple turns into a ball court with high stone walls and carvings of eagle-headed warriors. Spectators line the wall tops and risers at either end. A temple rests at one side, and in it, a stone jaguar sits. Priests gather at its sides and bear their jade-encrusted teeth. They're waiting, watching.

"To give one's blood to the Earth is an honorable and worthy death," Rafael says. "Are you worthy?" He looks at me, running his eyes over my body, and suddenly I'm no longer afraid of the waves, the drinking water, or even the saltwater crocodiles. I'm afraid of that look in Rafael's eye.

"The Mayan women . . ." He reaches out his hand. "They wear white dresses with bright floral patterns. The dress signifies purity and connection to the Earth. Are you pure, señora? Are you connected?" Rafael smiles and moves his hand over my sunburned skin, my neck, shoulder, the curve of my breast and waist. Salt water pushes into my nostrils, but I push the water back out again, and Rafael rests his hand on my belly. "Mothers who die in childbirth have a place in heaven."

What about mothers who kill their children in childbirth?

With his other hand, Rafael presents a necklace made of stone beads and seashells. He places it around my neck then presents another necklace like the first and places it around my neck, too. He layers the necklaces, one after another, weighting me until I can no longer move. My feet are like anchors at the ocean floor, and my arms drift gently with the blue turquoise water, churning, churning. At least I'm not caught in the waves.

I look down to see the stone and seashell beads and notice instead that my bathing suit is in fact white with bright floral patterns. Woman sacrificed, neither pure nor connected.

Figures.

Rafael turns as another man approaches. This man is smaller and bronzed. A mop of black hair drifts atop his head. He has a hooked nose like an eagle, and at either side sit eyes like almonds. Pieces of jade hang from his nose and ears. He says something, but I can't understand his words. We both look to Rafael.

"I don't understand him either. My ancestors were Aztec." Rafael turns in a huff, swimming away. Apparently, we have offended him.

The Mayan holds a ball up in his hand, and with the other, he points to a stone ring at the top edge of the wall. He wants me to put the ball through the stone ring. I've seen the movies; I know what they'll do if I hit this ball through that ring. I don't want to die, not like this. This is a man's death, not a woman's.

Did I say that aloud? The necklaces are so

heavy.

The Mayan points to the stone ring again, and I feel a length of wood in my hand. It's a bat. Damn, where did this bat come from? Mayans didn't use bats.

He throws the ball, and it wobbles through the water. When it pauses in front of me, I hit it. I hit the ball through the ring.

I didn't mean to do it. Reflex and all.

Applause grows in ear piercing waves, and the Mayan smiles. A jaguar priest approaches from the end of the court. He wears feathers and jade. His jade-encrusted teeth make me shudder, almost as much as the long flint knife in his hand, and he motions to the sandy floor where I kneel, no strength left for fighting.

Head down, I see the weapon's shadow. It lengthens then shortens as it raises above the priest's head, and I think, *this will be painful*. He won't be able to slice quickly with that blade. He'll have to saw and cut.

Survival for Artists: Blood Sacrifices

When the end comes, the artist will give up. No need to fight. Dying will be more beautiful for the artist, if she accepts her end. Then she can focus on the details of the experience.

Do it quickly. I think this but don't say it.

Honorable death . . . I can hardly hold my head up, and the priest is taking too long to strike. It's impolite to play with food and sacrifices.

The stone and seashell necklaces are so heavy.

I try to keep my head parallel to the sandy floor for the priest — might at least die well — but the necklaces pull me down like magnets to the ocean floor, and I rest my forehead against the sand. The necklaces slip off, one by one, and lighter now, a new wave, powerful, pulls me into its coil. The blade grazes my back, and saltwater stings at the cut. Blood and burning never felt so good, and air washes over me.

Air.

Survival for Artists: Second Chances

If life gives an artist a second chance, the artist should take it, kicking and screaming. This is it. Don't fuck it up.

"Help." I try to scream, but my breath is shallow. I'm back under water again, and the waves are moving me closer to shore. Sand brushes my feet. When the wave spits me out, I hear Peter's voice.

"You have to swim." He's close.

"Arm — "

"I can't hold you. You have to swim."

"I'm drowning."

"So am I."

I look toward the sandy shore and the rocks, all in a row. More strangers are watching us now.

"Help!" Peter calls, but they don't come. Strangers are too smart to help strangers when the water is dangerous.

"Give me your arm." I duck beneath the wave, but I'm a fraction too late, and it takes me with it.

Such a simple thing, an arm, but the feel of Peter's skin is like a deep breath of dry desert air, and he drags me through the water closer to him, closer to the shore. Treading.

"Swim!" Peter pulls, and I kick, pull, breathe. We climb our way toward the shore, but this is not a mountain, it is an ocean, so we tread, kick, breathe. The wave crashes down, and we duck, roll, kick.

There is a gulley of sand at the shoreline, soft, between the rocks, red flags interspersed between the strangers still watching us from the safe, dry sand.

The next wave comes — breathe, duck.

When we push up again, our feet are touching. Touching. Just barely, but finally touching. Breathe.

We cut our bodies sideways as the next wave crashes. The water rolls us, but when we stand, again, our chests are now out of the water.

Waists, knees, calves.

We fall in two salted and fleshy heaps, turning, panting, and watching the turquoise coils. The white foam tickles at our feet.

Yes, it's beautiful, but we are not romantics at wartime. We're lovers survived.

"Are you okay?" A deep, accented voice calls from behind, and Peter turns to answer it.

"You shouldn't ..." The rest of the man's warnings fall away into crashing waves and my heavy panting. I can hear Peter's tone, if not his words. He's agreeing with the man.

A great humility, it is, letting others see the edge of one's self.

The man with the deep voice walks on, whispering about "gringos" and "tourists." I turn to Peter, and see the fear and exhaustion on his face, the line between his brows. They are the same fear and exhaustion that most certainly rests upon my own.

"You didn't leave me," I say this without smiling. Death does not take its passing with smiles, but Peter smiles. With fierce eyes, the color of avocados, he smiles, still panting. Then he kisses me, and the saltwater tastes good on his lips. "You gave me your arm."

Never give your arm to a distressed treader. Unless you love them, only if you love them.

"Of course I did," he says this as if it was principle, a scientific fact. Love and science, they are not always so complementary.

Survival for Artists: Afterword

Survival is more beautiful for artists. It is a taste of death, a renewal of life. It is the essence.

We both turn to the turquoise coils and their foamy tipped edges, where, somewhere between them, we met our breaking points. We don't speak of it, edges and breaking, but we know the truth of it as we sit side by side and panting on the wet sand. We know the truth of it, and we share it in a squeeze of our hands. Another coil of water crashes to the earth. The echo of it pounds in our ears.

Rising slowly, careful of the ebb and flow, we start back to the resort beach just a few yards away, ignoring the straggles of spectators still watching us. We walk back to our children still playing in the sand with their resort club friends and Señorita Maria. We walk back to our lives, our blue and pink souvenir sombreros and plastic Mayan temple. Shame or courage walks with us. Perhaps both. Yes, it is both.

The kids are giggling and digging in their holes, and they wave to us.

"Mommy, look." My daughter smiles. "Can I bury you?"

Peter and I share a silent understanding.

"Me, too. Dad, you can get in mine!" Our son

grins, and both of them bat their eyelashes.

So Peter and I kneel, both of us shaking, unable to do anything but be near them. We do as they say and climb into our holes that they have dug for us while we were drowning. Yes, the irony lay palpable within them.

The children giggle, throwing sand on our bellies, and Jorge, the resort waiter, walks by.

"Margarita, señora?"

"Bottled water, please." And I take pause at the request before turning to Peter. "Do you know why we can't handle the water in Mexico?"

He isn't listening. He's laughing and shaking and gazing at our son. Precious time gifted.

"It's too rich," I say to no one in particular. "The water is too rich."

"I thought you said the water had poo in it." My daughter offers this much louder than necessary and throws a pail of sand on my legs.

"Yes, honey, I did, but I've learned a few things since we've come to Mexico, things I didn't know before, and on the point of water, I was entirely mistaken."

Fly Fishing In
Neoprene Legs

They wade through cool water currents and early morning air, around the bend and toward the old oak tree where he once played G.I. Joes with boyhood friends. On their legs, they wear Cabela neoprenes. They are clumsy, the waders, and she loses balance in the current.

He catches her like he had on their first date, *Psycho II*, when she slipped in a puddle outside the movie theatre.

Careful. He offers his hand, and she wonders if falling would mean driving back early to his parents' house where a warm fire and change of dry clothes wait in a suitcase or would he keep her here the full hour, cold and wet? *Something's biting beneath the dead oak, the one hanging over the stream.* He points, and she stares at the oak as if it is an enemy hoarding hidden treasures and fallen leaves and G.I. Joe memories.

It's a nice town. You'll love it.

I don't want to move out of the city.

It's just a visit.

From the woolen strip on his vest, he takes a dry fly — green and beige with dark brown striping made from dark brown thread, tied with his clumsy fingers while hunched over his father's desk. He and his father christened it, *The Big One*, at dinner.

He twists open a tin and dabs a fingertip into the salve. He rubs the salve on the green-beige fly like her Pappy had done so many years before. *Keeps it floating.* He explains then describes each step as he ties the fly to the fishing line — wrap the line, pull it through, careful, don't snap it. She does not tell him about Pappy. Maybe she never will.

He shows her two and ten o-clock, how to cast. She sees the same elegance of Pappy's withered hands in his grip while the line rolls out, positioning its fly beneath the dead oak tree. The current takes it downstream. At breakfast, between bites of scrambled eggs, he spoke of dead trees and currents and she moves to kiss him on the cheek because he is wise and can conjure Pappy images. Her thick wader legs splash.

Careful, babe. You'll scare the fish.

She stops mid-kiss, at the *careful* in his voice. She pulls a neoprene leg back not so unlike evenings she pulled a bare leg to her side of the bed.

He hands her the rod, smiling like a boy

offering a candy ring, because he is giving her his fly that he had tied with his own fingers. She casts. One, two, three flies in branch, in brush, in ear. He cuts the line while she watches, horrified she has hooked him. He curses and makes a big deal even though it was only the tip of the hook and the tip of his ear. The fly drops in the current, lost. He curses again. He is not so attractive this way.

The big one, he says.

I'm sorry.

He takes from his woolen strip a plain fly, one of a matching three he bought from the store. *Try not to lose this one.* He all but throws the pole at her not so unlike the times he's thrown sex.

She splashes. He doesn't hear. She splashes again.

Shhh.

She raises her right knee high, holds it so to put all her strength in its splash. The current knocks her off balance. She counts the ten seconds it takes for him to check on her even though she's called him twice.

His eyes watch her, though his waist faces the dead oak tree where several plip, plippings break the water's surface.

You okay?

I must have slipped on a rock —

Shhh. He turns to the oak again, and she pretends his whisper is for her, in some way that she cannot understand. For her, not for the fish, but he does not turn back to her. She splashes to the bank then strips angrily:

From waders (to release the water).

From jeans (to make a point).

From flannel and t-shirt (for good measure).

She stands — wet bra, underwear, woolen socks — shivering, moving as best she can into warm sunlight casted down through bare treetops. She calls to him, again, but he's caught the big one now.

A rainbow bright trout flips and shimmers, breaks the stream's surface then disappears again. He lets the line drag. He pulls it gently. He uses his fingers instead of the reel now, luring the big one in increments. His focus is complete.

If only he made love the same way.

He works the tie and hook from its mouth, carefully, to save it for mounting. He curses when the hook catches. He does not yell though his thumb bleeds more than his ear had bled. Leaving the hook, he turns to see her standing near-naked and shivering on the bank. He laughs, and she surprises herself when she laughs with him. He holds the trout up to show her the morning light reflecting aquamarine and rose from the fish's scales, and she knows what she'll buy him for Christmas this year — a scale suit with cut away genitalia.

He dips the bucket into the stream then lowers the trout gently, his tone apologizing: *Just a minute. Need to get him in water.*

Finally, he holds his flannel shirt like an overcoat, waits for her to slip into it. She smiles knowing he will collect the wet clothes and poles and bucket so they can walk to the car where he will hold the door for her while she sits on the faux wool seat. He will grab the fleece blanket he keeps for her in the trunk because the car heater has not worked for months.

He tucks the blanket about her legs and arms, making a fleece cocoon, where she warms herself and listens to the still flipping trout inside its bucket now gripped between her feet. She flips her fingers against her clammy skin in time with the fish.

Chinchillas

"Each smell has a story," he says then tells me of a special odor he's kept for years, high up on his shoulder blade. "This one's special. My lover left it on me." Addie scoots closer and onto the middle couch cushion, whispers, "Not a lover like wanting to be inside her, but a lover like wanting to be with her. We went to school together." He pauses. A moment that means I should say — *yes, yes, I remember her* — then speak out her name so to memorialize this lover and the odor she has left on his shoulder blade.

Blurred images of a plain girl in blue jeans, an oversized pink sweater, pulse hazily. I try to draw her images in my mind, push them into sharper focus. The moment grows awkward.

"She calmed me. Had a way of making the worst okay. Hurt like icy hot when she left. You know, on the balls."

I had assumed he'd left her because he had always been the prettier gender, the mallard with an iridescent green head, a yellow beak, the poet-musician with the perfect amber curl at the nape of his neck. Addie walked the halls strumming fingers on invisible guitar strings, moving girls' hips and legs and chests in time.

He hasn't lost it, not even a little. He shifts his hands, curls his fingers. They play air chords like Mozart on piano keys. He leans over, yawns, and funk vibrates from his armpits, adagios from his mouth, staccatos from his feet in yellow-orange waves of tone and melody. I resist the urge to move away from him, sit on the chair, give him the entire couch to make his music. But he is too beautiful, now.

He rounds his back to stretch again, circles his arms like a ballerina, settles into the couch cushion behind him. "We made plans. Real plans. New York City. Live like bohemians. Fuck like chinchillas."

I don't say rabbits.

"Chinchillas fuck meaner. Die easier, too. It's the cages."

"What happened to her?" Her. I have no name for the forgotten girl who fucked like a chinchilla and somehow the story moves into a faraway place, belongs to him secretly and I cannot access it because I haven't the key, the name of this chinchilla lover.

"Run over by a bike."

I almost say, *sorry*, or *that's sad*, or *wow, how random* but instead I do the one thing I hate and compare his chinchilla lover to a lesser, a distant

73

Uncle who was hit by a Harley, nearly killed.

"It wasn't a motorcycle. A bicycle. Schwinn ten-speed. Those things roll like NASCAR when they get going." Addie explains how the ten-speed clipped his lover at the bottom of a hill, knocked her unconscious. Never woke up. He sits straight, unbuttons his dark green jacket stained with darker spots of coffee? Whiskey or some other sort of alleyway drink? The nights must get so cold. He pulls at the top layer of shirts, rips the haze thermal, the dinged tee shirt, the sweat-yellow tank top. He pulls the layers down over his shoulder. "Here take a whiff."

I stand, move to the back of the couch so to study his shoulder better. His skin appears normal but for the faint red irritation high up on the blade that disappears into his dark greasy hair line.

"Blood splatter. I was able to brace my fall when the biker hit us, but it was all too quick for her. She hit the asphalt. Head splattered. I never washed it off. Can you smell it? Her blood? I can smell it. Every day I smell it. Every smell has a story." Addie pulls his shirts up over his shoulder, puts his coat back on and I envy him. I envy his memories like melodies, his chinchilla lover smell. I've never loved so fully.

"I should get going." He rocks to standing.

I make to stop him, put out a hand, consider

offering him a shower, a meal, a cup of fresh coffee then remember that I haven't been to the grocer's in over a week. I offer him a bowl of stale, dry Lucky Charms. No milk.

We sit with our bowls of Lucky Charms, watch the stark white canvas that has abandoned me, denied my brush for too many days now. Addie sets his bowl on the table then moves about the apartment, his arms and legs and odors wafting like ribbons in the air, dancing cavatina to our choir bites of frosted oats and yellow moons, orange stars, green clovers. So I open tubes of acrylic sunshine, burnt ember, coal black to mingle with his ribbon air. We open the windows — not to let fresh air in, but to share our symphony with passersby, the world en route. At night, we toast plastic champagne flutes filled with Carnation Evaporated Milk.

Sometimes, late at night, when the air is too clean, too empty, I join Addie behind his dumpster where we hum and wave our hands in putrefaction. I return to my clean bed in the early morning hours — unwashed, funk lingering on my skin — where I whisper Addie's melodies, imagine he and his lover in New York City. I lay and draw chinchillas in the air.

Art as Appropriated as Woman as Klimt

It is a cyclical actuality. Woman as appropriated through the eyes of a man's brush, at the tips of his fingers. Laid out on a couch. He sees her better this way. Woman laid. He stretches her on canvas. Draws her outlines with thin black paint and finds the curves of her cheek and breast and thigh, replicates her collective.

Klimt does a woman good. He twirls her with serpents. He gives her a penis and a scrotum. He shows her ass to the world and he says, World, see this woman's ass. It is full and subjectified and forever. It will remain, here, on this canvas, in my paint. I have signed it with my name.

He might have had groupies, Klimt. There might have been women standing at his door, throwing corsets, bending on knees, forming lips for the want of his signature on their ass cheeks. I might have been one of them. You might have been one of them, too. Imagine. Gluteus Klimti walking beneath skirt fabrics on the street, a wiggle and bump society, secret.

Come closer. Let's whisper, you and me. They meet Sunday mornings, the Klimti, behind the old woodshed, beneath the pear tree, in the back of your daddy's old Thunderbird.

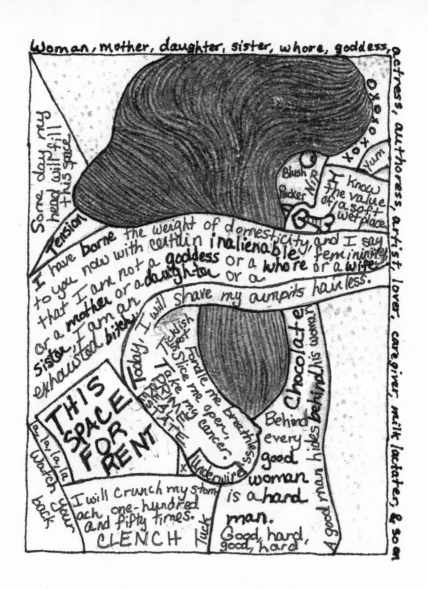

This Space for Rent

Gustav Klimt. *Die Leiden der Schwachen Menscheit. The Suffering of Weak Humanity.* 1902.

Coffined
Gustav Klimt. *Danae*. c. 1907.

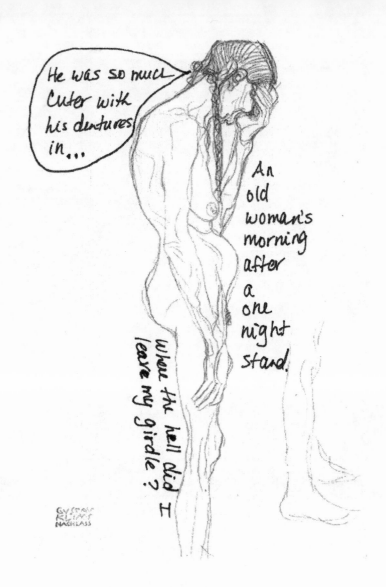

An Old Woman's Morning after a One Night Stand

Gustav Klimt. *Stehende alte Frau im Profil nach links. Staying Old Woman.* Date Unknown.

A Dream of Floating Women
Gustav Klimt. *Fischblut. Fish Blood.* 1898.

Goldfish Have
Hot Sex

Gustav Klimt.
Goldfische.
Goldfish. c. 1901.

Deus ex machina — Color her zombie. Make of her mouth your flesh and blood. Tell her she is the future of all things then buy her an x-large Slurpee and a black lace thong and six-inch hair extensions. TELL her she is beautiful because, really, she will believe you. Tell her that her cravings for mind and clarity and logic, her own checking account and the perfect brain freeze are unfeminine, evil heretical and all things unpatriotic. Leave her alone — yes, with herself — wanting more.

Deus ex Machina

Gustav Klimt. Gorgonen. Gorgon. 1902.

83

She gives good head.

Hairless like a little girl.

This is not pornography. This is classical art.

This Is Not Pornography

Gustav Klimt. Allegorie der Skulptur. Allegory of
Sculpture. 1889.

Arch, arching, arched.

Ooo, Baby!

I will stand here, in this position, for hours. I will flip my hair and wind my hips. When you come to me, I will scream and scratch and make you think you are hurting me because you are so long and wide and rough...
I will say, fuck me, harder, then wait for you to fall asleep, when I will breathe you nonexistent.

Bent

Gustav Klimt. *Stehender Mädchenakt mit vorgebeugten Körper nach links. Staying Female Nude with Bended Body Heading Left.* Date Unknown.

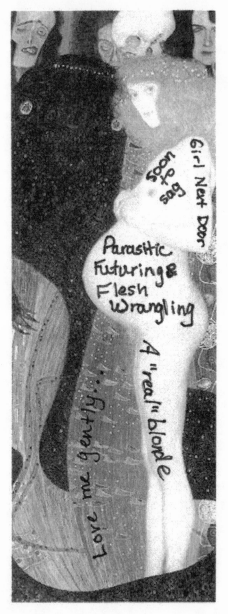

Parasitic Futuring

Gustav Klimt.
Hoffnung. Hope.
1903.

PEACE
JOY
SERENITY
A bud
in the hand
is worth
two in
the bush.
The Interior Clichés of Women
- All these bitches are wearing my dress.
- Trans. "What a lovely frock we share."

The Interior Clichés of Women

Gustav Klimt. *Chor der Paradiesengel. Choir of Heavenly Angels*. Detail from Beethoven Fries. 1902.

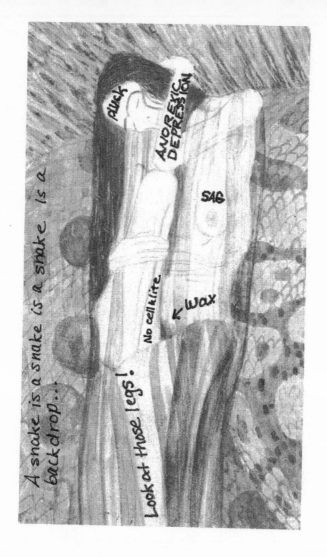

Anorexia Cavum

Gustav Klimt. *Nagender Kummer. Gnawing Pain*. Detail from Beethoven Fries. 1902.

Solipsy Street

I imagine you. Not the real you. The other
you. Your body sweet and golden as if made from
butter and flour and sugar, the pieces of you sun-
baked in a muffin tin. In my mind, you sit on a
window ledge, cooling in the breeze. I pull you
from your tin lathered in Crisco and flour, form
your limbs and torso and head together, glue you
with cream cheese icing. It is easier to imagine
you this way, sweet baked and sculpted, an edible
man walking the street. I imagine crinkled muffin
wrappers on your feet. They match the banana
yellow short-shorts you wear, the ones I had given
you on your last birthday so we could laugh
together, again. They stop me, the short-shorts.

Your black duffel bag shifts as you step off
the curb and cross Mount Avenue toward Solipsy
Street. You wander along the sidewalk to nowhere
particular, it seems. Street hopping. Left, right.
Right again. Left. I cannot make out your
directions. We are lost, nonexistent and traveling
through nevermores, shortcuts that haven't
happened because they aren't supposed to have

happened. They are alleys transcendental, erased before acted. Disappeared like bad things in good suburbia.

Where are we going, today?

To a hotel.

Will I like it there?

No, but you have to see this. I need you to see this.

The hotel lobby is dark and littered with needles and rat shit, an occasional whore in a peek-a-boo costume. One wears Underoos, blue with white stars. They are so happy the Underoos, and I silently thank her for her efforts at levity in such a dark place.

Your banana yellow shorts suit the lobby in a cheap, want to fit in way, and I crave a shower with you so to lather your skin against my skin. You speak to the clerk, fetch a key and I notice the clerk is eating a banana. The peel drapes over his fingers, and I realize your shorts are not banana yellow, after all. They are lemon meringue.

I owned a yellow bike with a banana seat once, remember? I told you about it when we were still new. Told you about how I wrecked it while peddling in strong winter wind on road ice. A cookie sheet caught in the spokes.

Why were you riding a bike in the winter while holding a cookie sheet?

My mom needed it delivered to the neighbor's house. Couldn't wait. Christmas cookies for a Christmas play.

Why didn't you drive?

I was eight.

Why didn't you ask someone to drive you? You always settle. You settle like bad yeast in too heavy bread.

I know.

We walk up shag-crusty stairs. The fibers are the various colors of gangrene if gangrene could infect carpeting. It would make better sense to walk downward, a gangrene stairwell leading us into a basement wound, but we walk up as if to heaven. The carpet should be blue or white. I mourn for the absence of pretty carpet.

You leave the door open, absently, without turning or stepping to the side. You are ignoring me. I follow in leopard-printed slippers, step on soft ball feet—toe, ball, toe ball....

Quiet. Flatten into the wall, into the dirty papered wall like submerging into buttermilk. Nose, eyes, round of my belly, the fuller pieces of me peaking out, milk drenched, because I can no longer pull them in like I used to. You sit on the stained floor mattress in the middle of the room. She wears a shiny, yellow, pleather skirt. How lovely, the matching. You know how much I like when things balance. A needle hangs from her arm. She pulls, closes eyes, drifts the needle to your hand, and you drop it accidentally between your thighs, carefully fish it from the crevice of your flesh. Push the needle beneath the mattress and I imagine it is for safety, so you won't prick yourself. Your kneecaps are so bony. I must feed you beef and mashed potatoes tonight, seven grain bread.

When you fuck, your legs are like albino eels, long and smooth, the crotch of your banana yellow short-shorts pushed to one side as you slide on the condom, push up her skirt. I imagine you are made of muffins again, you and the girl stuck together with cream cheese, and she grabs at you behind her, pushes her face into the mattress, breathes so hard I think she might asphyxiate. Her arms are bruised, beautiful. Yes, she is that too. I will give you that. You have chosen a beautiful whore. But—and I only say this for aesthetics' sake, not to be cruel—for the front teeth. It is so difficult to tell the ages of your junkies.

The room chills when you leave. I tell you simply for your knowing. This time, you will know how the room feels after you've left it. I wonder, sometimes, how the room will feel when I'm gone. Maybe you will whisper it to me late at night. I will be a ghost hovering over you.

She lies small on the dirty floor mattress, and I go to her, make to lie down, cover her and fold my arms about her waist, but I'm still wet from the buttermilk wall so I study the corners of the room, check the bathroom, peak behind the door. Anything. Shirt, towel, something to warm her, but there's not even a plastic shower curtain to cover her with. You have left her cold on the floor mattress, dripping. It is sad.

I might have spooned her then, cradled her warm, but I would only make her wet. I cover her with the twenty dollar bill you left, place it gently on her shoulder.

We walk the street back to Mount Avenue, turn right toward home. You stop part way, walk into a coffee shop, slow and crumbly. A broken muffin man. A woman watches you disappear into the bathroom hallway. Minutes later you return wearing a gray suit and tie and black leather shoes. I wonder if your short-shorts are in the bag or did you throw them away like a ticket stub?

You order mint tea. I should have known it was tea. I had wondered about the peppermint and bitterness so many evenings.

We travel home, you and I, slip through the front and back doors respectively. I glance in the mirror—sunken cheeks, pale skin. It won't be long now.

Where were you?

Gardening.

What's for dinner?

Porterhouse. On the grill? Would you like that? Thought we'd have mashed potatoes, too. Seven grain rolls? I made muffins today. We can have them for breakfast.

Sounds good.

We sip buttermilk on the back porch and do

not talk about doctors or sex or ends. We discuss
starlings and blue birds and the tomato plants. I
mention canning the tomatoes with basil and
garlic, homegrown sauce for the winter.

Perhaps we can give them out in Christmas baskets.
We'll see.

We watch the sun fall behind wood fencing. A
finch, yellow and black, lights on the magnolia
flower that has lost its petals. The bird's tiny feet
cling to the dead, woody stamen and I almost ask
about the girl, almost say, Should we check on
her? Take her a plate of leftovers? But you pull at
my hand, squeeze, swing our palms between the
chairs. In time, when the wind slows and the
finch no longer rustles between the leaves, I can
almost hear the crumbs of your fingers falling,
landing on the wood deck beneath us.

Spyro Gyro

Clear plastic circles beneath my pen of
iridescent turquoise flutter-shaping on
your skin.

Buttercrisp

Buttercrisp crackers are divine. When I crack one in half, buttercrisp crumbs fall between my legs and to the floor and the man who lives in my closet crawls out on his hands and knees to eat the crumbs.

He followed me home one day after I refused to walk through his open door. He stood holding it, waiting for me to go through. I played with him, making little jerk movements as if I might actually go through the door, stopping short each time so that he jumped a little each time. He laughed and I laughed but I wouldn't give him my phone number or my name though I did give him long tongue kisses when he did not expect them. He followed me everywhere after that.

He was pretty. Briefcase, gray suit, dapper blue tie. I let him take me to lunch and we ate marmalade on buttercrisps and alligator crepes then washed it down with honeysuckle wine while laughing out loud at other people's jokes until the people moved away. That was our plan.

He asked for my phone number three times

96

during lunch then stalked me home. I flipped up the back of my skirt, showed him my Monday underwear, *Monday's Knickers* written across my ass cheeks with little red lip kisses along the waistband. He tried to be sneaky about the stalking, hiding around corners and behind pedestrians.

My mother said never to leave the door open, but I never listened much to what my mother said, so I left the door wide and pulled the left-over buttercrisps with marmalade from the doggy bag then crunched and sprinkled them in a trail to the closet. He followed the marmalade sticky, crumb trail, curled up beneath my winter coats where the other men had lain. On the top shelf were my hat boxes in shades of pink and lavender, filled with childhood pictures that might have explained why I like buttercrisp crackers and store men in my closet. We don't open those boxes.

The other men I gave away to girlfriends, but this one I keep. When I want to play with him, I pull a fresh bag of buttercrisps and my man runs out of the closet, away from the gray-suited bed he made. He wags his tongue, romping playfully across the floor so that I giggle and coo and scratch his belly. I say sit! And he stands. Roll over! He nuzzles at my ear. Some nights I even let him sleep on the bed, though he prefers the rug by the fire, so I crumble buttercrisps and trail him

to bed where he licks marmalade from my finger,
sometimes I lick from his.

Collecting Calliope

The attendant washes her porcelain limbs, careful to hold them with fingertips. He lays her, disjointed, on black shag carpeting — arms, legs, head — inches from the joints of her torso. He calls her by name, "Calliope, Jigsaw Lover." Then sings to her a happy Camptown tune — "Calli, Calli, musing girl, duh-doo, duh-doo…"

Footfalls sound in the stairwell, and the attendant stops then turns to watch the man named Tiresius — though his name might be oracle or sage or Bob in this century. His friends call him Prophet. He grips the banister as he descends, running his left palm and fingers against the wood. When a splinter edges up, stabbing his palm, he neither shudders nor pulls away, but instead holds tighter, focusing on the slow bass booms between palm and wood, vibrations from the stage above. It is the place called Chance, where the man's dolls dance, Venus girls with pink fur and wily legs.

Another splinter catches, and this time, he pulls, finger to lips, where he sucks on the tiny

wound. It tastes of sweat and oil from the hands
that have followed this same banister down, down
the stairwell:

To the black velvet room
Beneath the dark city,
The place where
All come to play.

Prophet walks into the velvet room where
stars play over his skin and long, slicked hair,
darker than it should be for the centuries he has
lived. He cannot see them, the stars, the attendant
or the velvet curtains, but he knows they are
there.

The lantern stars swirl, and he holds out his
right hand to where a star drifts down then rests
on his palm. Prophet lifts it to his ear. *Who will we
puzzle tonight?* the star asks. "Whoever walks
through our door."

He pushes the star up, a five-pointed
butterfly. It flutters to a velvet wall. Prophet claps
his hands. "Ready, get ready." And the attendant
closes three sets of stage curtains.

The first client leads a pimple-faced boy,
perhaps fifteen, who watches the toes of his shoes
as he walks, tracking glitter and pink tufts of fur.

"No good will come of this," Tiresius

whispers to the fluttering star by his ear. *Quiet, you ancient fool. We need the money.*

"We've come for your talents," the father says, and he clenches his son's shoulder.

"Welcome." Prophet gestures to three velvet chairs.

Now, the dolly show begins . . .

"Gentlemen." Prophet claps and black curtains part, revealing a stately woman. She is clean and manicured and spritzed with rosewater.

A nameplate sits at her feet. It reads: Ophelia, The Courtier, in Copperplate Gothic. She wears an ivory gown, lighted behind, so that her hips and breasts and curves of her thighs shadow against the gossamer fabric. In one hand, is rosemary, in the other, thyme, and over her shoulders, fall dark waves with rose buds and ivy. She gazes to the floor — a good, shy girl — but when she speaks, her lip crinkles, suggesting her to be a knowing lover.

"My Lords."

Twitters sing from the black velvet walls, as if made by a chorus of fairies or maidens or lantern stars. Prophet raises a hand to silence them.

Another black curtain opens — The Huntress — a beauty with bronzed skin. On her shoulder hangs a bow, on her back, a quiver. Leather pulls tight across muscles, tendons, breasts. Her eyes,

101

amber glowing, pierce the men.

The third curtain opens for Calliope, a perfect specimen in height, weight, hip to bust ratio. She wears neither clothing nor hair, but for that on her head, and it hangs long in wide, blonde ringlets.

"Interchangeable." Prophet nods and the attendant grabs Calliope's scalp, pulling the blonde, replacing it with red.

Ooh, aah! The chorus stars brighten.

The attendant sticks his finger into one eye, then the other, and pops the orbs from their sockets, replacing blue with green. Then he positions her arms out, palms upward and stands back so that the man and his son may observe.

"She is all metal workings," Prophet says, "bronze and copper cogs with rare, precious gems." He leans closer. "Smooth porcelain outside. Between her legs, velvet, where she vibrates when you touch her there. She is named after the epic muse."

The father chuckles then turns to his son. "The tart or the muse?"

The boy does not answer.

"Time to make you a man."

The boy looks at his shoes.

"Perhaps," Prophet says, "I may offer another."

Yes, yes! The chorus stars swoon.

A curtain opens and out walks a man, young

and smooth.

"His name is Alexander."

The father screams, the boy grins. "He'll take the tart," the father says.

The attendant leads the boy to a room backstage. The father watches Calliope.

"Will you taste of her talent?" Prophet says.

The father's eyes narrow; he shakes his head.

"She is delightful. I must tell you, an everywoman for everyman, a puzzle lover if you'll forgive the expression. She'll teach you lovely new positions." Tiresius leans closer and whispers into the father's ear. "She can be disconnected like a doll. Just last week, we had a bachelor party who delighted in her disjointed features. It took us three days to put poor Calliope back together, but the men paid a divine rate for their pleasures."

The father licks his lips.

"We can give her a handle if you wish. One for the back of her neck and one for the small of her back."

The attendant leads him to Calliope's curtain.

"Father, I've done it!" The boy's cheeks are glowing, and he searches the room. "There." Prophet points to Calliope's curtain.

When he pulls back the curtain, revealing his father, the boy's eyes return to his shoes. The chorus stars laugh, the boy runs away, the father dislodges Calliope's handle. He sits her down gently on the carpeted floor, where limbs and head already lay, then he pulls up his pants, shrugs both shoulders and follows his son up to the boom boom stage.

"Puzzle lover." Tiresius smiles.

The attendant sings while collecting Calliope — "Calli, Calli, musing girl, all the live long day." He wipes each piece with soapy water, dries her with soft cotton towels and kisses her fingers, kisses her toes, before putting Calliope back together.

Street Red

He says lie down, take off your shoes. He points to the velvet couch. It is soft violet like warm spring evenings after the sun has fallen. Above it hangs a mirror, long, gold, gilded, screwed to the ceiling. The mirror captures me with skin stretched smooth in dormant repose. Laugh lines forgotten if laughing is the cause of them; I cannot remember. My hands are to the side, legs drawn over three cushions, too firm, so I float on them like Jesus on fairy tale velvet.

My toes wriggle from the coolness. They are restless, my toes. They want to walk, cover, hide their chipped red paint, Street Red, the girl had called it, as if assuming my toes might crave the feel of a street late at night, wearing black leather, stiletto heels walking toward a car sitting idly, purring, beneath a streetlight, flickering. A man sits there, in the front seat, watching me, watching him. *Meet me around the corner,* he says.

Such work would be easier. Simpler, I think, though I would never admit it.

"How was the week?" the doctor says.

"You always ask me that."

"And you always say 'You always ask me that.'" We both pause because the session has started badly.

"It was long and tedious, a boring desk and a Post It incident."

"Post It?"

"Don't ask." I pull the skin back at my temples, and my eyes disappear in the folds. "I don't like seeing the effects of it in your mirror."

"The effects of the Post It incident?"

"The effects of my life. Is there a camera behind it? I mean above it?" And I squint trying to discern dark spots in the reflection, a tell of something above the glass.

"Does that concern you? Cameras and mirrors? You've asked before."

"And you haven't answered me."

"No . . . no mirror. What if there was?"

"I don't like this angle."

"Maybe's it's not the angle you dislike."

"You're right. It's me."

"So imagine yourself another way."

Squinting again, I let the workaday reflection fade and try to imagine myself as Street Red, but all I can manage is a princess in pink taffeta then a cheerleader with pompom hair. Next I am a mannequin lying in a velvet box, a present, a plastic jewel. The wrinkles fade, as do my skirt and blouse and bra and panties. Next fades the

106

pink of my nipples, all genitalia, then the muscles of my arms and legs grow stiff. I can't move my lips, but they are so lovely, like rubies against alabaster skin.

"Good," he says. "You're making progress." And the tone in his voice is knowing, as if he knows me better now that I am plastic and sexless and motionless lying on his couch of velvet, and I want to tear him into pieces with my Barbie hands.

He makes me lay in plastic for the hour or what's left of it, watching my reflection in the gold, gilded frame. Gradually in small increments, I come back to me — a sag here, a flush there, after while my lips loosen.

"How was it?" he says, putting a hand on my thigh still bare as my clothes have not yet resurfaced.

"Enlightening." I try to hide the agitation. Try to move my hand to push his hand away because his fingers are too close, too familiar on my naked thigh, but I haven't the use of my limbs yet.

"Well, it is a process. I can write you a prescription — "

"No. I don't need one." I smile. "It's helping. Thank you. I see better what I should be, what I want to be."

He studies my face, and I smile, again, hoping it will pass for what he expects of me.

"I'm glad to hear it."

Clothed, sitting, shoes back on, I turn to him before leaving. "Is this who I am? Plastic, smooth and pretty?" And as I say it, my shame is there, but so is a wish for these shallow things. To be what is expected of me might make the days easier.

"It's who you want to be," he says.

"I thought I wanted more. There was a time when I wanted more."

"Perhaps there will be more, in time. Patience. The mirror will help you see it, but I think your perception has developed nicely so far."

And as I step through the door, I pause. Turn. "What do you see, doctor, when you look into the mirror? What is your perfect reflection?"

"I don't look into the mirror, dear girl. I haven't the need."

City in Spires

Timmy pushes the thin cover down over his legs that are welted and scarred from flea bites. The mattress is bare and stained beneath him. He scratches at his ankle and ignores the stain though he must feel it. It is wet. Yes, he must feel it. His eyes are dull blue, red-lined, as he tips the glass. The last drop of milk runs down and into his mouth. He turns to me.

"There isn't any more." I should tell him to clean himself, to clean his mattress. He'll stink before long, but it is no way to begin the day.

"Will we eat, today, Addie?" he says. It is the question I dread each morning.

"I'll find us something."

"How do you know?"

"It's your birthday. Ten-years-old, a whole decade. We need to celebrate." I quiet my voice, soothing is better. "You should wash up."

Timmy's eyes cast downward.

"You want to look good for your party don't you?" I don't have the heart to mention the urine and the smell and the dark wet stain beneath him, though we both know it's there.

He smiles and tries to stand. His body is thin and he falls back to the mattress. "Mom got me a present."

We both turn to the long, motionless form strewn sideways on the couch, her face pushed against the dirty grey cushions. She hasn't moved in two days, save the toilet and a bite of bread and she cradles the bottle of gin that I had given her two nights ago. I found it propped in a dead man-beast's lap. He had been sitting in the alleyway leaning against the red, pocked brick, a day gone, by the smell of him. Mother hugged me when I brought it to her, a good hug like she used to give, then she slept not restless and mumbling but a good sleep, coffin still, as Mama Reenie used to call it.

"Do you think it's a glove?" Timmy's eyes water. The glove is more than a nice-to-have. It is a necessity for him. I try to smile, but my lips are thin.

"We'll have to wait and see, won't we?" Today's list: food, glove, another bottle of gin. "I should go. Promise me you'll stay inside." I pull his chin up so that he has to look at me. "I mean it, Timmy. It isn't safe for you outside."

"But you go outside."

"I'm an adult."

"Only just." He pouts the way he does when he knows I might give in, when I might let him do as he wants because one of us should be allowed to choose.

His lips are cracked and white than usual. I can almost imagine them pink.

"When you're eighteen, you may do as you wish, but at ten…" I stop short as eighteen echoes through me like days left and forgotten in the bottom of a well. To see Timmy at eighteen. "Just mind me. Maybe later, when I'm home, we can take a walk together."

"You're not my mother, Addie."

"Might as well be."

We both turn to the couch again.

"Promise me." I take his chilled hands and rub them, pulling his fingers close to my lips. I inhale like air before drowning then blow the warm belly air onto his thin fingers. They warm for a moment then cool again. His fingers. I can never keep them warm. "Promise me, you'll stay put." I stick out my cheek, and he kisses it. "Wash up and put on your sweater. It's chilly this morning."

Timmy grabs the dingy, wool knit balled in the corner where the aged wood floor meets the peeling sage green paint of the wall. "We'll play ball," he says. "When he gets back, he'll want to go into the field and we'll find a ball there—"

"You know dad isn't coming home." It's harsh, but Timmy forgets sometimes and he needs reminding. He needs to know what will and will not be.

Timmy nods, but the glove and baseball still sparkle in his dull, blue eyes.

"Maybe we can go to the park together later. See you soon."

"See you soon."

Goodbye is a word we don't use anymore.

On the street, I breathe fully, letting the outside air clean the stairwell dirt and the urine and decaying rats from my sinuses. The sun has already cast its glow and the homeless are waking. They mutter and his as they mark their territories between boxes and shanty fences made of trash piles in rows. Sounds of urchins drift from the alleyway, and Mrs. Sentry crawls through the heavy lid of her overturned garbage bin. She pushes at the giant metal door that swings creaking on its hinges above her. She nods, her mouth still stitched together with fishing line. Tomorrow, they'll remove the stitches. *After she's learned her lesson.* Though, Mrs. Sentry has never been one to learn her lessons well.

Across the street, urchins scowl at each other, pulling at opposite ends of a whimpering dog. It is a mutt of several breeds, too wiry and unkempt to know which, and it struggles between their hands. The smaller boy has hold of the dog's hind legs, and the bigger boy has hold of its head. It is tired, the dog, and it turns toward the noises of the children who stand to the side, egging the boys on while the sun filters down onto the alleyway, that scene of scabby young and stinking puddles that splash and soak into their' tattered shoes, into the mange of the dog's coat as it hovers the boys' gripping hands. They are lucky ones, the boys. With a quick snap the dog falls limp and the smaller boy drops its legs, conceding his loss like the smaller part of the wishbone, and the other boy whoops and hollers with delight. The children descend upon the dog.

I almost turn right and into the alley. It would be a good meal for Timmy's birthday, but I haven't the strength to fight them all off, so I turn left toward Prospect Street. Meat from the park is better, I tell myself. Maybe I'll find a pheasant or quail.

A clockwork spire sits at the corner of Prospect and Sycamore overlooking the park below. It is a shifty thing like an amalgam of watch bits, a titanic timepiece smashed apart and welded together again, giant iron cogs and wheels on a flagstone base. The iron pieces move fluidly, as I approach, more like water than mechanism, each piece connecting to other, melding, reforming and working its wheels back and onto itself, making abstract, monochromatic shapes —

dogs, buildings, trees. It is a limitless kinetic sculpture. It has moved for others, too, but often, not recently. People talk. *There's something not right about that girl.*

Mr. Hadley sits on the cracked sidewalk, propping his back against the stone base, his little tin cup beside him.

"Good morning, Mr. Hadley."

I lean against the base, too, where I can observe the park and the pond below. It is still and clear and void of the duck shit and muck that rimmed its banks years ago. Now it is only a reminder. No fish, no foul. A symbol of want.

The tall, yellow grass moves at the pond's edge. A rat, maybe. We must eat today.

"Still scraping, little urchin?" Jenna leans against the flagstone base, too, clicks the heels of her tall purple boots against the cracked sidewalk three times.

"Still hoping for a tornado?"

"Hoping for Oz." She pulls her fingers through the length of her long, brown hair then lengthens her back, straightens, yanks the front of her shirt down to show her breasts better. "Hoping for something." She winks.

I point to the left bank. "Something moved in the grass."

"You don't have to scrounge, you know."

"I'm not that desperate."

"You will be." Jenna takes hold of my long

braid. "There's a special call for reds. If you'd just let me fix you up a bit. You know . . ." She runs a hand down over my waist, my hip, pauses there. "We could make enough money in one day to feed Timmy for a month."

"Is that your father's idea?" I don't try to hide my contempt. He had Jenna on the streets early.

"It's not so bad, Addie. You get used to it."

"Used to strange men fondling you?"

"It isn't exactly fondling." She scratches at her thigh through the black net stockings. The stocking rips. "Shit." She turns, strutting down the sidewalk. I drop my bag by Mr. Hadley's tin cup, take out the short kitchen knife and prepare to hunt for rats when the spire moves again into the shape of long-necked birds.

"Wouldn't that be nice?" I nudge Mr. Hadley's thigh with the toe of my canvas sneaker. "Mr. Hadley, I'm leaving my bag with you. Mr. Hadley?" I nudge him again.

He mumbles and arcs his head but instead of telling me to get lost, his eyes grow round, and he points to the sky where a flock of Canadian Geese fly into the park.

The crowd is silent. Heads turn from the spire to the geese that now move in gaggles around the water then back to the spire.

"Strange happenings here." Eyes cast down in

115

the Reverend's presence. "Geese?" He stops beside me, and the group takes a step back, giving us room. "Is this your doing, Adeline?"

"The spire formed them then they came," I say.

"Strange."

She is a strange child, unholy.

"Miss Adeline, we've not seen you at service in some time."

"Did you hear me? It took shape then minutes later, the geese flew in. Mr. Hadley saw it, too."

Omen...prophecy...magic...

The Reverend turns to his assistant — a small, golden-haired boy in matching white robe, gold cross and dark eyes. The boy runs off, and the Reverend turns back to me. "You'll not do this city favors by conjuring stories, Adeline."

"I'm not telling a story, Reverend. I swear to it."

"Swearing is the practice of deceit."

The boy returns with the Mayor and takes his position again beside the Reverend.

"What do we have here?" the Mayor says.

"Seems we have a magic spire." The Reverend laughs the way men do.

Magic...food... gift...

The Mayor considers his constituents. "Now,

now. I'm sure there's a reasonable explanation."

"The girl," the Reverend points to me, "she says that the spire made this form just minutes before the geese appeared."

"Is that so?" The Mayor considers the spire, the geese, me.

Food...food...food...

The Mayor laughs. "Looks like we've been given a gift, Reverend. Dear girl, how did you make it work?"

I almost say it isn't mine. I almost say that I didn't make the spire move, that it has moved for others, too. "I don't know, sir. It just moves for me sometimes."

"It moves every time Addie's near it. She has a way with spires." Jenna offers, and I shake my head at her.

"It's true. The spire moves when Addie's near." Mr. Hadley is now standing. He puts a hand on the stone base to keep from wobbling.

One by one, the constituents claim their geese while the urchins skip along behind them waiting for scraps.

The next morning, the crowd waits by the spire. They stand in a circle, parting as I draw near. The Reverend and the Mayor are there, too. Everyone waits quietly.

Mrs. Sentry moves from the circle and puts a

hand at the small of my back. She smiles and the faint lines left by the stitches fade. "Go ahead, Addie. Show us how you do it."

I take my place close to the spire. The crowd makes room and ignore the Reverends warnings of parted waters and chariots: "Look to God for signs of prosperity, not this girl."

I can feel his gaze. I know it well. *No one guards a secret like a child.*

This time, the constituents sound off in turns. "What if she touches it? Can she make it bring food? Push her. Push her to it." They move closer, inch by inch, closing the circle. My chest rubs against the iron clockwork, and instantly it starts into motion, the same fluid melding of metal churning into its new form.

The Reverend puts a hand to his mouth. "Witchery." But the constituents do not hear him. "Witchery!"

The constituents do not shift.. They focus on the spire and the sky. They listen for wings and wind, but when the spire settles again, the metal pieces do not form geese but four-legged creatures.

"Are they deer?"

"No, they're buffalo."

"They're too skinny to be buffalo."

"How do you know what a buffalo looks like now?"

The crowd turns to the park where a herd of

twenty some deer file into the tall tufts of grass. They settle and graze and the constituents speed into collective action grabbing their nets, knives and rifles.

That night they build a bonfire and drink turned wine and laugh and sing and make up verses: "Addie, Adeline, girl of our dreams...."

Timmy dances among them like a hummingbird between wolves. He dances with color in his cheeks.

Mother rustles when I wake her.

"It's morning, Mother. I'm going to the spire. I'm going to conjure meat today."

"She can." Timmy joins in. "Addie can conjure birds and deer. Everyone sings songs about her now."

Mother opens her mouth with rancid breath. She drinks from the bottle in her hand. "I was a conjurer once," she whispers. "I conjured men and love and beautiful things. Oh, how lovely they were. Did I show you my gowns, Addie?"

I lay a hand on her shoulder. She turns back to the dirty cushions of the couch.

"Can I come outside tonight?" Timmy asks.

"After we've built the fire." I kiss him on the cheek. "Don't forget to wash and put on your sweater. There's some meat left in the kitchen. Eat it before it goes bad. Give her some." We

119

both stare at the couch.

The Reverend and the Mayor argue today. The Reverend walks grimly away.

"I don't know how you're doing it, my dear," the Mayor says, "and I don't care. Just keep at it. Your gifts are our salvation." He claps me on the back then walks into the field among the freshly killed bear where his constituents carve fur and flesh. It is a joyous scene.

That evening, we dine on bear meat and left over venison. Some of the women talk of seeds, a vegetable garden and apple trees.

"How do you do it?" Timmy bats his eyes.

"I don't know. I don't think it's me doing it."

"But it happens when you're around. When you touch it."

"I know."

"Can you make it turn into a baseball glove?"

"I don't think it works that way, Timmy."

"But you don't know. You said you don't know, so it might."

"Maybe." I smile and pull the blanket up over his now rounded shoulder. It's good to see fat on him.

The crowd of men have gathered. The women no longer come to the spire but instead prepare their kitchens. It is Timmy watches the men, studying them.

"Timmy," I say, "maybe if we touch it together. Maybe then it will give us what you want. Think of ball gloves, Timmy. I will, too."

When the spire forms into dancing and playing children, I pull my hands away. Timmy and I fall silent and wait with the men for the dancing children that we hope will be dancing cows or sheep or goats.

We can hear the children minutes before the walk out from between the buildings and down the streets toward the park. It is as if they don't see us. They run, jump and swim in the pond. They are clean and lovely and they don't seem to notice that we're watching them, or they don't care.

A strain rises palpably through the crowd, in the men's whispers and cocked necks.

The Mayor steps forward. "Don't worry." He laughs and turns a sideways glance to me. "Touch it again. See if you can fix it."

The spire reforms upon itself. Another set of children appear joining the first.

For six mornings, the children appear. New groups added to the old and each day the children grow weaker and slower.

"They aren't supposed to be here."

"We haven't the food to feed them."

Fighting and stealing break out amongst the homeless first. On the tenth day, we see the first child floating in the water.

"They're dying."

"Look how thin they're getting."

On the Eleventh day, apulpit has been set beside the spire. The Mayor takes his place. "I have considered our hardships. The children are a mistake. This we can agree."

"Yes, yes, we didn't want them."

"They aren't supposed to be here."

"It's all her fault."

"An unholy, unholy mistake." The good Reverend, his cheeks now gaunt, his eyes blazing, reclaims his place beside the Mayor.

"The spire has been misplayed. We were promised sustenance, survival, and what we've been given is a curse." The Mayor and Reverend both nod. "We should never have trusted such work to a girl."

When they begin rounding up the children, Timmy and I scream. We run, try to shoo the children away, but they are too weak. The constituents stack them by the bonfire and tie me and Timmy to the base of the spire.

Timmy cries.

"Shh," Jenna says. "They'll make you be quiet

if you don't stop. Don't say anything, Addie. Just look the other way."

"They're children. You can't do this! You're murderers, all of you. You're the reason things have turned so bad!"

The Mayor nods to the Reverend and the Reverend nods to his boy with the golden hair.

When Timmy sees the stitches, he cries for me. I would tell him it's okay. It doesn't hurt as much now.

When the bonfire dies down, and the constituents have filled their bellies, they walk past the spire to their homes. They cast their hatred and guilt and blood-soiled mouths at us.

Weeks later when the stitches have left their faint red marks on my lips, I leave Timmy on his mattress and mother on her couch and walk into the sun again. Mrs. Sentry crawls out of her garbage bin and smiles. We nod to each other, a silent sisterhood.

The urchins play in the stinking alley, tearing at another stray dog, the sun highlights their tattered shoes that are wet with puddle water. I pause at the alleyway looking beyond to where my spire still sits. I will never touch it again.

I turn into the alleyway. With one jerk, I pull

the dog from their grips. The urchins back away from me whispering:

"Careful, or I'll conjure you in the spire."

They scatter, leaving me alone in the alley with the dog now limp in my hands. I sit it gently upon the cracked and puddle asphalt, stroke its matted fur. It limps out of the alley and turns down the street and I watch it safely on its way. The children will not hurt it as long as I'm watching the dog. They're afraid of me now.

The dog turns back to consider us all just once then makes its way out of the city, wagging the nub of its missing tail.

I Keep a Vine Woven Basket by the Front Door

It sits like mahogany veins twisted into themselves — a hollow of wooden pulmonary. Beneath the basket rests a Rubbermaid wet mat, sky blue, and I lay in it my twisted head ripped from its shoulders, snapped from its spine. Afterward, air moves freely like the removal of too-tight ruby heels at the end of the day. I have no business wearing such things on such days. Ruby heels are for gold brick days.

I sit the head in the vine woven basket to drain. Its neck oozes tensions from busy drive-sits, wait-sits, stuck-in-traffic-and-rage sits.

Drive the poor dog laying so still in its cardboard box bound for the child-sized cemetery with stones stacked teetering on the other end of town. Find a pretty place on the edge. Where there is no headstone. Dig. Dig with the rusted spade that he left. Sit in the dirt and cry with elbows on knees bent so that you can smell the fresh turned earth. Cry so hard that eyes blur and face streaks black with mascara dripped into the hollow of a button shirt stained white to gray, and the black runs down between narrow breasts making a black line to the horizontal lip of fat rimmed at the wool tweed waistband. It tickles. A low rumble jiggles the box making the air smell of kibble. Dig. Lift the cold body, now firm, from the box because the cardboard is somehow unnatural. Lower the body gently then drop it because the depth is too far to reach. Sit some more with face pushed against sweaty palms filling with blisters, these hands that just dropped a dead friend. And no one will ever know. Lay, on top of the body, a card that reads Lily — *Lily, child of mine. I did not know you. Here you can rest with a friend* — and dig into the already dug pile of earth, chopping at clumps of sod, wishing the frost hadn't yet come so the digging would be easier. Pour the dirt onto the golden fur. Pour the dirt onto the card that reads *Lily*. Pour until they are gone, the dog and the card, the card being the worst because it is made of snow white linen paper. It had to be snow white.

It is a man's job, digging. A hard job.

Yes, I said it out loud, inside my head.

Go home.

The sky blue mat turns crimson from the bloody thoughts dripping out of my head. By day, sunbeams shine through the transom window and bake the blood. By week's end, the basket and mat stink of digging and dropping things and menial things, too, like *yes, that skirt does make your ass look big* and *no, I can't come to your party because I don't know how to talk to you; I don't know how to talk to anyone* which leads back to the digging things: *Stop your damn dog from barking because I don't have time for barking dogs that remind me of the one I held in my arms, stroking its golden fur while the veterinarian injected poison into its veins, and while you're at it, keep your children inside because they remind me of the life I've lost, and I hate you because you don't know these things. I hate you because I hate myself for not knowing how to tell them.*

On Saturday, I'll hose the mat down; let the blood of the basket and the mat wash out and into the backyard grass, into the dirt for the earthworms to eat. Then I'll scrub the mat with Clorox bleach. My fingers will turn raw and pink. The basket? I'll spray it with Lysol, citrus scent, even though I know the blood will still be there. By Monday morning, when the antiseptic and citrus odor fades, I will smell the blood as I walk out the front door.

But the blood keeps oozing, and Saturday is four days away. Like steamed asparagus, blood rises in mists dewing the skin of my head's cheeks and the antique mirror above it, tinting them both pink, so I remove my head from its basket and wipe it with the green, white-checked dishtowel. I never liked that towel anyway. He left it behind when he moved out, when I pushed him out, when he left me because I needed him to leave.

While screwing my head back onto its neck, I sit on the bottom stair and watch the deep crimson thoughts laying in the mat steam up in swirls, like mists from a mountain top. They rise to the ceiling then hover, turning to crimson clouds. They drift down, a fog scented air, like copper coagulate. I'd rather they rain. It's so much better to let blood pour, easier to clean. Foggy blood sticks around much longer, fills the air, and my air filter no longer works.

I grab the crimson mat and run to the kitchen sink dribbling blood along the way, slipping in it, catching my balance just in time.

Leave it. I'll clean the spilt blood later.

The mists swirl as I poor the blood from the mat and down the kitchen drain. I run hot water, but it makes the swirling worse so I turn on the disposal.

The crimson mist rises, a whirring cyclone from the disposal's black rubber flaps, and it tries to pull me into the metal teeth of the drain, catching my fingers in the swirl. I resist, gaining them back to me in small increments. The cyclone is too strong, so I drop to the wood plank floor like a soldier clawing at an arsenal and open the cabinet where the citrus Lysol sits, but I can't get the cap off. My hands slip, misted with cyclone blood. What did I do with the towel? Wiping hands on wool tweed slacks, bought on sale at Macy's, I try to dry them, but they won't dry completely and instead turn sticky, grip the cap, and I yank it from its can. I spray Lysol with slashing strokes of citrus mist, and it cuts the crimson cyclone like ghost swords. Three, four, five strokes and the cyclone fades away, replaced with antiseptic gashes in air, wounds of long, lingering happy smells with a hint of antiseptic. A clean aphrodisiac, so I spray a little on my wrists and inside the crooks of my elbows.

Time for bed. I'll clean the blood tomorrow morning.

Over the white porcelain sink, I remove my face. First the eyes, then mouth, nose, the rose of my cheeks. Finally, my hair, and I clean the blood from it with Suave apple-scented shampoo. I sit these all on tiny shelves behind the medicine chest mirror.

Hands out so not to trip, I make my way to the gilded ivory dresser by the hickory sleigh bed. It is pearlescent like oyster gems. I open the top drawer first where I rest my drained and faceless head. Down the row, a drawer for each part: one for breasts, one for waist, one for my hips and

129

ribs and legs. My feet go in the last drawer. I have skipped the drawer for my womb, vagina and clitoris. They have had such a rough day, so I keep them with me, cradling them beside what is left of me, more mist than soul, singing a lullaby, then reciting by heart a story of wild things in wild places and wondering if such places might really exist outside a child's head. I promise that we'll visit the wild things next weekend when work isn't so heavy. I promise, though we both know that we'll not have time or energy. My womb smiles anyway. She needs to hear that we'll try, and the mist soul smiles, too. We snuggle closer. I hold them lightly so not to add further to their bruises. Tonight is for cuddling, and I promise to be patient with them, to listen. We don't speak of the day, the week, the clinic or the vet.

Loss in twos is really too much. Really, it is.

I wake each time they shudder or cry like lost doves in the spring, and I am patient still. I listen and wonder if there might be time to visit the wild things one day when all the pieces of me heal.

I'm lonely, my womb says between snuffles, and I say that I know. There, there sweet girl, I know. *Will we ever be full again?* she asks.

I feel my way through the dark and to the bathroom faucet where I fill the small glass with water then feel my way back to bed.

Drink, I say.

I don't want it.

It will help you feel better. Please.

She opens her mouth and takes a small sip.

Why did we do it?

He wouldn't have stayed.

He might have.

He's already gone.

You pushed him away from us.

I had no choice.

That's what you always say.

Her name was Lily, I say. I buried a card with her name on it. I buried it with Princess to keep her company.

I like Lily. Maybe we could have another, and we could name her Lily, too.

No. One Lily is enough.

How about another Princess? And we both look at the end of the bed where Princess had lain the night before, the weight of her muzzle over my ankle.

Maybe.

I miss him.

Me, too.

Can we find another one of him?

One day. One day, we'll look again.

Do you think we can find one who doesn't snore?

Yes. I can't help but giggle. Yes, I think we might be able to find one who doesn't snore.

That would be good. And my womb turns over, inching the round of her curves into the round of mine, and there as sleeping forms drained of the day, we rest the way of tomorrow, when again, on the sky blue mat, our losses will lay.

Man-Beast

A partially trained triped who looks good in a pair
of Levis.

Postfeminist Zombie Assassins Wear Wonder Woman Underoos

He can't see the red, white, blue and gold set hidden beneath three layers of cotton button down, tweed and the gray wool overcoat. She smiles, closes stretched and bruise red lips over a glass of neon-green appletini, sugar-rimmed.

She sets the glass on the make-shift party desk, letting the edge of her hand rest on plastic-wood coating even though it smells of coagulated beer and happy hour parmesan cheese bits. She stands, left leg on floor, and picks at the polyester panty wedged between ass cheeks, grasping at elastic edges through tweed and Hanes hosiery, getting most of it, accepting the rest as stuck.

He gives her time so not to embarrass her or come to her too quickly, so not to stifle the image of this strange dark-haired temp with bruise red lips, picking. He wonders if she is like this all the time, able to perform intimacies in crowded after-work office spaces with suits and ties and attachés like uniforms around her.

He moves closer to this girl-woman, still digging and watching those closest to her, stopping if anyone's glances move toward her. Starting again. He stops three desks shy so to fix another appletini, salt-rimming the plastic glass. He asks the nerdy tech guy, who is good for such things, to deliver it. He grins.

She accepts the drink, nods, gestures for him to approach, giving a flourish of hand and fingers that could mean confidence or aggressiveness. Her cheeks have a flush to them. He can see it now. The flush matches her bruise lips in a charming and natural way, and he wonders if her cheeks flush like this all the time or if it is because of embarrassment, wondering if he had seen her picking.

Thank you. She gestures to the appletini.

You're welcome.

She sips through bruise red lips, registering neither surprise nor disgust at the salt-rimming.

He had wanted more. A declaration of sugar preference, an indication of independence, a cringe, something, but she does not declare herself independent of the salt. She is a true temp, an adapter. She accepts the salt, drinks from the glass a second time, careful to sip from the already mouthed section of rim so to avoid new salt. She is a follower, mannerly, and it disappoints him a little. This one, he had thought, was a true blue ass picker. He had wanted her to be a true blue ass picker.

Do you prefer Romero or Boyle? She does not elaborate on the names or their meanings nor does he ask. Her face shows disappointment. He shrugs. They stand, waiting for another *in*. He tries talking about numbers. She tries Shelley. He tries the Lakers. She listens, adapting.

When they leave the office together, she tells him she doesn't usually do this and she's a little bit nervous and maybe he ought not to expect too much of her.

He offers to take her home, cringing at the ought not in her sentence even though it doesn't sound so bad when his buddy says it and he wonders if he's a hypocrite, a little shitty. A small release of her shoulders triggers a calm in the car space, as if his offering was all she needed to hear. She says: No, I deserve this.

He smiles, encouraged. Maybe she hasn't fucked in months, years. Maybe days. Maybe she's a wildcat. She deserves a right rolling, all right.

By the way, I liked the salt, she says this not watching him but instead watching the blur of lights and neon storefronts pass by the car window. She says: The salt was nice with the sweet.

They stand, bedside, and he pushes gently at her shoulders as if to indicate: take off your coat, lay back, let me do the work.

I prefer the other way, she says, and she moves, adapting her body to let him lay down first then she sits on top of him, straddling, letting the gray wool coat fan out around them. Square shoulders, puffed chest, she is a shero ready to disrobe.

I want to show you something, she says, and he feels himself hard already. First, you have to promise something. She puts a finger to his lips as he starts to agree — yes, yes, anything. You have to promise you'll lie completely still.

I can lie still, baby. It pops out though baby is not usually his way. This girl woman has a baby way about her and he cannot help himself.

No, I mean it. Don't move an inch. Stone still. Dead.

He nods, remembering the short, blonde waif from college who liked to play dead. For three nights straight, she lay still, feigning sleep, waiting for him to enter her, no sound when he pulled down the boxers he had loaned her, the underwear beneath. He could still hear, sometimes, the little moan she let escape, as he slipped inside her.

His chin moves to his chest then stops. Stone still.

She pushes to standing, feet at either side of him, wool coat now down over shoulders like a striptease, bend at the knee, unbuckle, unzip, pull his pants down. Rip open his shirt. He is stone still. Mostly.

When she stands over him, hands on hips in Wonder Woman Underoos, her bruise lips purse, unmoving — they do not quiver or tighten or tell of embarrassment. She is all Wonder.

I'm glad I found you, she says. I had thought I'd rounded you all up, but here you are hiding. Do not try to resist.

He almost nods again into his chest but now he is in complete awe of her.

I liked the salt, she says again, as a whispered aside as if breaking her character too loudly might break the mood and so she offers this quiet aside as a reminder to him that she is woman and not a superhero or an assassin. She winks.

She pulls the tie from his neck, unfolds the knot, pushes it roughly into his mouth and ties it again at his left ear, just below the lobe. There is a tenderness in the way she puts two fingers between the gag and his cheek.

So you won't bite. She dismounts, walks to the closet, thumbs through his hanging ties, chooses an electric blue with Snoopies and Woodstocks, a conservative red and white stripe. It matches, she says. He nods, agreeably gagged, though the crimson red and navy blue are much darker than her outfit. She ties his hands to the iron bedposts.

I am the postfeminist zombie assassin. Do not

try to escape, she says.

He watches her, eyes wide, pulling to test the ties, but subtly so that she will not see his nervousness. He tries to remember if they had agreed on a special signal, safe word, secret handshake. Just in case.

From her attaché she pulls long red boots and a whip, spray-painted gold, chipped in sections. She slips bare feet into boots, zips, smoothes hands up to knees. She coils the rope, running her right palm over the golden length then pulling it section by section into her left where she grasps it until the length of it lay in neat rings, collected by long fingers. With one long snap, she releases the coils into air, bringing the whip down hard onto the floor.

You've been a bad zombie. She flips her long dark hair and he imagines that she wears a Wonder Woman crown at the crest of her hairline. He decides to buy her one.

I'm going to teach you never to bite again. And her bad shero lines vibrate in tones through air and her fingertips on his chest. He tenses like a boy-man fresh from a Justice League comic convention defending the Wonder Twins as two separate individuals even though they metaphorically represent the same nature. They have different powers, though similar.

I'm not a zombie, he mutters through his tie gag.

I did not give you permission to talk, zombie puke! She whips him, hard across the chest, for his insolence.

He mumbles something, incoherent even to himself, just to feel the golden whip across his chest again.

Again.

He mumbles and writhes, aching for her because he is the bad zombie caught and gagged and waiting for Wonder Woman to fuck his brains out so he can eat them like a good zombie.

When she leaves, he is still tied to the bed. She says nothing, walks through the door, hidden in gray wool.

He thinks of her each day, while punching numbers and shopping Ebay for a Wonder Woman crown while his supervisor isn't looking. At 5:01, he checks the temp lists. At 5:08, he walks to the nearest bar. By 10:59, he readies himself to walk home. 11:00 is his limit. Backtracking home, he watches for her, the girl-woman and her attaché filled with golden whipping and red boots. His Wonder lover.

Paddlehead

He serenades me from his suicide ledge while juggling paddles with little pink balls still connected. I ask him to come inside, laughing a little bit, and he thinks I'm laughing at him a little bit, trying to hide the sentiment.

The pink balls bounce off his head while he sings — *I am a paddlehead, ooh yeah*. And I sing melody to his base — *Paddlehead, paddlehead, come on home*. Though, I will still leave him anyway.

I'm hungry, he says. Did you make brownies? Will you make me brownies?

I'll make them if you come inside.

If I come inside, you'll leave then I'll jump out the window. Suicide requests are compulsory, burdensome, especially when they involve cooking.

We sing through the morning and into the afternoon as I feed brownie bits from a cloth napkin, red and white checkered. We drop chocolate crumbs on passers by then laugh when the passers look up to see who dropped crumbs on them, seeing no one because we've flattened ourselves against the building, hidden by a three-inch ledge. This has always been Benny's world, brownstone edges.

I convince him to let me cinch him in with bungee cords. I'll leave if you don't, I say.

He lets me hook him by a series of cords through the window, attached to our wrought iron bed.

Two days. No one has seen Benny on his ledge yet. This is good. The police would turn Benny's transgression into a newspaper deal, ten o'clock news, months of hospital intakes, outtakes, insurance deductibles and paperwork. Benny is proud. He has me and he knows it.

He grins a brownie-eating, lip-stretched grin. *I am a paddlehead, ooh yeah.*

Benny, come inside.

I bounce and bounce and I take you down with me.

Benny, it's cold and I can't bounce. I'm only a girl-woman.

He asks me to kiss him, so I kiss him, slipping an extra bungee hook into a loop of his blue jeans that are actually black, except where they've worn gray at his knees and groin.

Caught you looking! he says.

I wasn't looking.

Yes, you were, you were looking at my package, my gladiator, my zip-it-down taker.

Benny, I'm tired.

When I push him into the air, he falls back,

arms wide, bouncing off the building like a suicide ball against brownstone.

I love you, he says. She meant nothing to me. If you leave me, I'll die.

Pulling out of the parking lot, I pause at the curb to watch him bounce slowly now, close to the ground. He could unhook himself easily and jump down to the sidewalk, if he wants, but he dangles instead, hooked to his bungee cord, arms outstretched and singing — "*paddlehead, paddlehead, ooh, yeah, be my paddlehead gal.* A woman walks by, and Benny clings to her, his hands and feet wrapped around her arm until she swats him off. He springs back against the wall, bloodied and broken.

I park, walk back to him, pull him down and unhook the bungee from his jeans loop. Benny, you have to stop all of this, I say. We climb the stairs and eat brownies in bed until night falls again. Then I bungee Benny to the bed after he's fallen asleep.

I check on him three times a day. Bought him a guitar to keep him company while I'm not there. The neighbors sometimes complain, but it keeps him happy. He sings — *I am a paddlehead, ooh yeah. I am a paddlehead* to my tape-recorded melody.

Paddlehead, paddlehead, come on home.

[Jeezus] Changed
My Oil Today

Jesus. Not [hazoos] or [həzoos]. [Jeezus]. He
wore blue rubber gloves and a matching Lube
You shirt, cotton, with a half sun on the left
breast pocket. Introduced himself as [jeezus]. In
his right hand, he carried an oil wand. With his
left, he popped my hood, pumped refined amber
clean into my oil receptacle. I don't presume to
know the exact name of my oil receptacle. It is a
mystery too rich for me like knowing the rate the
earth spins on its axis or how fast a hummingbird
can beat its wings, when exactly a soul will leave
its body upon death.

Jesus knows the name of my oil receptacle.
He might even know the rate of the earth's
spinning. He is a rich-looking young man. Wise
blood. Civilizations behind his ethnicities.

He might know why the Maya fell, the degree
of Fahrenheit and Celsius that turns water to
steam. Mechanics know more than they let on.
They are walking common-wikis, clearing houses

of everythings. Mechanics know these things because no one expects them to know them. The Law of Unknowing, like Murphy's Law or My Aunt Lucille's view on life that she shares every July family picnic — *You'll never know more than you're meant to, in life, unless you're a know-it-all, a lawyer or a mechanic.*

Maybe Jesus is nothing more than a glorified window washer, an attendant with a vehicle checklist. I can still see him in the thin space between hood and frame, the horizontal section of his blue Lube You shirt crinkling and folding while he checks my belts, tops my fluids, rattles my wiring. Jesus knows more about my workings than I ever could.

Is she oiled? Check.
Is she rotated? Check.
Are her wires connected? Anti-freeze filled? Check, check.

Jesus bends at the waist, stretches to reach plugs, connectors, popped off caps, peers through the thin break between metal roof and metal frame. He winks at me with meaning, and I imagine that I'm thirty years younger and he's crawled up my skirt, peeks out now between elastic and skin, a burrowing Peeping Tom, a snoop in my medicine chest. I might have looked away, pulled knees together, crossed my ankles, but some part of me wants Jesus there, peeping beneath my hood.

My knees fold out, rest against door and console. I've never sat so wide-open before and I imagine that I wear a hot pink mini-skirt instead of these denim pedal pushers that cover these goddamn varicose veins.

It is satisfying, Jesus under my hood, popping and topping and I begin to giggle, a little at first, but then it turns to outright laughing, and I imagine he has a line item on his checklist for each part of me — brain, heart, kidneys — all the organs of me there on his checklist, a special section for the special places that never seem to matter much anymore.

My husband is not amused. He sits in the passenger seat, watches me peek through the thin open space between hood and frame. He squints and breathes heavily.

Jesus is changing our oil, I say.

My husband turns, stares out the window.

Would you like your ticker checked? Brain flushed? Penis recharged?

He ignores me, and before I can think of more cajoles, Jesus taps on my window glass. That will be twenty-three, ninety-five, mam, he says.

I've rolled my window down for him and now I can smell the oil and grease on his hands, the cologne he must have bathed in that morning.

146

How hard he must work at covering the scent of vehicles and fluids every day.

How much for my husband's heart? I wink at him.

Jesus tilts his head, crinkles his brows.

Hasn't had a tune up in fifty years.

Laughs.

Really, he could use a little help.

My husband sighs, and Jesus squishes his lips. I've made him uncomfortable now. He takes my money, smiles, gives me my change, waves me on my way. Have a good one, he says, then turns, oil wand in his hand, waits for the next customer to drive into his bay.

All You Bad Sinners

Grab a straw. Do it. This isn't an exercise in the mind. I want you — yes you — to go to the kitchen, rummage through the drawers, grab a straw, hold it in your hand. Now, fill a glass or a cup or a coffee mug with bubbly like Coca-Cola, Sprite, seltzer water, champagne if you have it then come back, sit down, start reading again.

Get up. This is not a hypothetical exercise.

Got it? The straw and the bubbly? You wouldn't cheat, would you? You're not sitting there grinning at the page and thinking, *hah, like you'll ever know.* I do know. We all know. Get the hell up, go get the bloody straw and fill a glass full of bubbly.

Got it now? Good. Let's get started.

* If you're cheating. If you're sitting there without the straw thinking you've gotten away with it, curses on you. Curses on you and your family and the little dog you plan to buy in the future after you have children or the children you've had move away or you realize you don't want children

at all and end up lonely so you buy a little dog to cuddle. You cuddle it. The minute that little dog runs into the road and gets hit by a car, you'll think back to this story, and you'll say, *Holy shit! I should have gotten the straw.*

Now. Stick the straw into the bubbly.

Sip. Slow-like. Let the bubbles fizz at your tongue tip. Pull the bubbles back through your mouth and feel the fizz. Let the fizz move into your sinuses and imagine you can see the bubbly flow down your throat. Follow it. Imagine that the bubbles are all the bad things you've ever done.

Yes, you've swallowed them, all those bad things.

They're in your stomach now. Like the time you called your mother a bitch but wanted to call her a whore. The time you stole your best friend's Barbie doll then dismembered it while imagining it was your best friend. They're there, all of them inside you, quite literally, bubbling in stomach acid. The day you wanted to hit your girlfriend for calling you dickless but instead pissed on her toothbrush while she slept. That's in there, too.

What? Your bad things are worse? Well, you've swallowed your worst then.

Take the straw, stick it up your nose.

The definition of a coward is one who is unable to face fear and mistakes and bad and worse. Cowards are afraid of little plastic straws.

Straw safely planted? Good, let's continue.

It is believed by some that flagellation will refocus attentions, wash away sins, but flogging leaves long, nasty, red marks. Psychiatrists, not so historically, believed in cutting connections between the frontal lobes. Effective, but still, this was a permanent and brutal practice. Shock therapy has always been the most effective of such methods, but psychiatry sessions and hospital stays can be expensive and not all psychiatrists are willing to use shock therapy nowadays.

Listen. The bad in you sits in your stomach now. It bubbles in acid. Let the bad bubbles and acid fill you. Let it pull you to moments when gray turned black. Moments when nasty words tasted good on your lips, as did the connection of your fist to her jaw. The desire of the girl so small she didn't understand.

Now sniff. Hard and long. Take it full in, push it back out.

This is your conscience fix. Your home remedy shock. Keep your straw close. Find a special place for it where you can get to it whenever you must. Keep one in your car, in your bedroom, make a straw sculpture to perch on your work desk so to remember. Sniff bubbly morning, noon, night. Keep it handy, a synapse douche for those times when your brain doesn't feel so clean. Sniff and imagine the bubbles are tears, collected. Imagine they are the little girl's or your mother's or your best friend's. The stranger you never knew. Imagine you can put the tears back, make them never-happened. Imagine tears sipped through a straw by a little girl's lips, and the tears were really your own only you were too young to understand. Sniff as if you could take back your sins.

As if you were never a sinner at all.

Stiletto Dance

Dance, girl, dance on tiptoe stiletto, hinged, oil knees and quivering. Lay neck to pole, balance.

Slide.
    To.
        Floor.

Crawl to the man with the twenty dollar bill, show breast tip, suckle-cracked shimmering in disco starlight and painted. Strawberry gloss. Show him and grab the bill before he pulls away.

Turn.

Crawl to the suited couple in disco light, laughing into Blackberries. Unfold petal legs, knees and thighs. Watch his hand move to her and her hand, too, as they watch you and laugh and sigh and rub while whispering of figures and market gain.

Dance, girl, dance.

Inch like inchworm to the little man, upstage, wearing wig and dark glasses workaday expression. Gritty end to another cattle day, and his mouth speaks of eagerness and sex and roses, possibly red. Will he come again tomorrow?

Slide, girl, slide a pole, across stage with legs wide. Exposed. Slide, girl, slide.

And dance where the stiletto beat tap, taps on stage. Dance to the flamenco, hard rock bass. It wears leather tight melody.

Dance, girl, for me on a sweat-covered stage. Dance for your rest behind curtain. Dance for the little boy waiting at home for birthday cake and action figure, for life worth living and dancing on stage if living life is worth the trouble.

Dance.

Cow Tipping

When viewed from a distance of years and circumstance, a simple poker game between friends becomes a machination of rubber bands and twisty ties, reminisces about high school football and Jack Daniels, cow shit in the moonlight where, after many a Friday night, good ol' Marrow boys have stalked a heifer named Miss Molly.

Miss Molly belonged to Fred's daddy who was a farmer like his father and his father before him. The family owned dairy cows since before Confederate soldiers raided the fields and barns of Marrow Valley. When Fred decided to go away to school and become a psychologist, not a farmer, it nearly killed his daddy, but Fred was determined, as most Marrowian children were, to get out. Find something bigger.

When his daddy, years later, lay in bed, sucking on canned air, Fred and his wife Genie left DC and Fred's fancy Dupont Circle office to return home. The cows needed feeding and milking, fields needed tilling.

Fred buried his daddy in the family plot beside his mother and an old Cottonwood tree that stood way back in the field for generations of Fred's family. The cows didn't shit so much back there and it got a good wind on most days, from the east and over the wheat fields, so the country air turned more sea than manure and a person could sit on the little concrete bench and stay a while, contemplate the rolling hills and rocky ridges, cool like pudding between the stove and the fridge. His mother had made good pudding.

He renovated the goat barn into an office, sold the cows and sublet the fields to another neighbor who had secured a government furlough. He built a little shed up by his dead parents and kept a small patch of farm for himself so to plant pumpkins and a corn maze in the fall, because he might have kids one day. Genie never cared much for the country or kids, but they had a yard now and a yard meant kids so she stayed with Fred. Eventually, they had Petey.

Petey was a smart kid.

Poker night most often convened in Fred's farmhouse cellar. He renovated the cellar into a modern poured concrete space and bought a fancy poker table with four comfortable chairs and a beer tap that read Budweiser. He hung a red and green and blue tiffany lamp low over the table and a sign on the cellar door that read Man Cave, a Christmas present from Genie after he built

Genie a laundry room on the main level so she would never have to go into the Man Cave.

No one ever considered the possibility of holding poker night on any other night than the first Monday of the month nor did they ever consider bringing anything but Budweiser and whiskey. Jack Daniels or Wild Turkey. Jack preferred.

Fred turns to the sideboard cabinet that sits against the wall, opens one of the small doors and pulls out a fifth of Stolie. Sam, Jim, and Alan stare at the bottle.

"Well, looky here. We've got ourselves a Russie." Jim nods to the Stolie bottle as if making its acquaintance. By the end of the night, he will have named the bottle Vladimir and given it an American alias, Toby, and assigned it a sexy full-chested Russian spy girlfriend named Nadia who is really an American nuclear weapons expert and wears red lipstick and has a hankering for CIA agents from Lynchburg, Tennessee. Particular for agents named Jack.

Fred tries to put Vladimir back into the sideboard again.

"Uh uh. You've done it now, Freddy. Keep him out." It's not that Jim hates vodka or Russians. He's been known to sip Absolut a time or two on lunch breaks. The issue is imprinting, symptomatic of the cold war years when Vans and skateboards and old fallout shelters were the in.

"Maybe I can interest you in this." Fred slips his hand into another cabinet in the old sideboard and pulls out a stack of light blue envelopes stuffed full and cinched with a big rubber band. Fred unwinds the rubber band slowly, avoiding eye contact. Jim, Alan and Sam watch him grinning. Fred keeps all his bad deeds in the sideboard. It is his only way of getting back at Genie.

As part of Genie's concession to move from DC to *bumfuck*, as she called it, she and Fred struck a furniture bargain. If Fred consented to an entire household of new furniture, she would move to the country. Genie spent a week in Crate and Barrel and a month later, Fred's disheveled farmhouse turned into a successive maze of showrooms. Bedroom, kitchen, living room and dining room complete with a brand new, Crate and Barrel Christmas cover, distressed barn wood table and matching sideboard with a tall corner cabinet which was far superior to the Fred's mother's Victorian sideboard.

Fred had won the 1989 Marrow High School Wood Works Competition for a rocking chair he'd made his father then given to him for his birthday. The rocking chair and sideboard both ended up in the Man Cave.

The sideboard was dark oak with curved paw-like feet, ornate brass handles that *wasn't rustic enough*. In truth, it wasn't the physical banishment of the chair and the sideboard that bothered Fred so much. Fred liked having the rocking chair in the Man Cave. The sideboard was functional. It was what the banishment suggested. Fred's mother's sideboard was by extension, his mother. She was a rough-hewn woman who gave her children attention in short bursts of fury and disregard.

In all fairness to Fred, his mother was a loathsome woman, even for a farmer's wife. Cold, hardworking, a farm wench who all Fred's life spouted orders like a foreman, laid love like a harness. "You done good work, boy," was the best he'd get on his birthday. With enough whiskey in him, Fred still, after all the years, tells the story of when he was a ten and woke early and made his way out to the barn to milk the goats, Nan and Ninny. When he stood, an hour later, in the cold farmhouse kitchen, his pants milk-soaked, his hands holding two half-spilled pails and freezing, his mother cursed him for being wasteful and clumsy. Eventually, something snapped in him. Alan, Sam and Jim could see it. One day he showed up to Marrow Valley High, before homeroom, red in the face and shaking. He wouldn't say what she'd done or said that time, but later that night, they followed him to the field and up the hill where Miss Molly stood. He put his hands up as if to tell them, leave this one to me boys, then turned and stared Miss Molly down for the better part of a half hour, Jack Daniels in hand. Before long, he swerved in and out, between the heifers then, when he was in five feet of Miss Molly, threw the empty bottle over the hill, bent down into a three-point stance and railroaded Miss Molly like the end of time was chasing him. He hadn't worn his boots. When she tipped, Miss Molly broke his ankle and kicked him in the head at the same time. He was lucky he wasn't killed. By the time they got him to the ER, Fred was covered in his own vomit and blood, cursing his mother and mumbling about milk pails and goats.

His childhood rested upon that consistency and so the sideboard represented something he'd never be able to fix or have back again. His youth and his mother. His resentments lay in peripherals he'd not be able to grasp and negotiate, which was a damned thing for a head man. By banishing the sideboard, his wife banished him by extension, struck him out of his castle, sent him to the dungeons. Genie had effectively revealed all three of them—mother, son, sideboard—for what they were. Outdated. Unwanted.

It might have been funny but for the generality of it all. For Fred, it was the sideboard. For Jim, it was his father's vibrating corduroy

Barcalounger. For Sam, his antique typewriter collection. For Alan, the first computer he had ever purchased with his own money and a tall metal black CD stand with a silhouette of a Jazz player on top.

Now, twenty years later, Fred's mother's sideboard is the group's collective act of sustainable vengeances against their wives.

Jim hides his collection of *Penthouses* in the top right drawer. Sam hides his *Hustlers* in the drawer below it. Alan's weed is in a tin that he keeps in the bottom of the side shelf. Cigarettes, which Fred had promised his wife he'd quit, lay in a Tupperware bowl sealed inside a gallon-sized Ziploc. Bottom drawer is where the whip and handcuffs lay like a joke, should anyone's wife get out of hand. The worst deed of all, Ms. Ruskin, lay hidden in Fred's collected light blue envelopes gathered with the rubber band.

Ms. Ruskin's letters lay on the card table now. Fred pulls one letter from the stack and opens the envelope, lays the letter with a photograph on top of the green felt. It's a picture of Ms. Ruskin butt naked except for a garter belt and a giant Flintstone's Dino stuffed animal between her legs. At the bottom of the polaroid is a message written neatly in small, black letters. *Miss you.*

"She's a freak," Sam says, "though, she'd make a splash in the morning addition." Sam never misses an opportunity for news or gossip.

"You can't keep her all to yourself for long, Freddy boy."

"Yeah," Fred grabs at the photo, but Sam won't let him have it and instead passes it to Jim. "She grades Petey's homework on the bed."

Jim, Alan and Sam all stare at him.

"Maybe, if you work real hard at it, you can fuck Petey's way through middle school."

Most men who went to Marrow Middle School can still recount which of them had been caught red-tipped beneath their desks. Ms. Ruskin had and still has extraordinarily large breasts. When she writes the morning vocabulary words on the blackboard, her breasts jiggle out to the side where her arm and hand reach up with chalk, writing ever so tirelessly her vocabulary list only to find that she's erased half of it by the end. The boys wait breathlessly to see if she misspells a word or writes it sloppily enough that a boy can raise his hand. *Ms. Ruskin, is that a W or a U.* They take turns like their father's have taught them. Ms. Ruskin's boys have been the winners of spelling bees in Marrow County for two decades.

"You going to see her again?" Sam asks.

Fred grins.

"You are a dedicated father, Fred. Don't let anyone tell you different." Sam smacks him on the back. Everyone raises a glass, drinks.

Sam opens the box of cards and deals them. Tiny pictures of naked women flick out and onto

161

the table top.

"Oh Shirley." Sam has named the redhead who sits backwards on the horse, legs spread wide and leaning back in the saddle.

"Say, guys." Alan says. "What do you think about Jarod joining us one night."

Jarod recently moved into the old Smith house down the street with his wife and two little girls, also twins. Alan had never lived so close to another family with twins. It was comforting, knowing that another man with twins lived close by, as if Jarod represented a potential ally the same way a man might become a borrowing buddy on Saturday afternoons when your weed whacker has gone bad. Just walk across the street and ask the neighbor for his. The twin factor connected them as if their sperm was made of the same stuff.

Sam sets the ante and calls the game. Seven card stud. The men take a sip of their beers and/or whiskeys and stare at the naked women on the backs of each others' cards. When they've picked up their hands, Fred starts.

"I'm sure he's a nice guy." His tone is one who states the obvious but holds back, ready to give some other detail that will make the obvious less appealing.

"I'm sure he is, Fred." Jim holds his cards inward. This is Jim's tell. He overly guards his hand when he has something good. He's holding at least a straight. "Might be nice to have another player." He discards one card. Sam gives him another.

Fred grimaces, takes a swig of his beer.

"I just thought it'd be nice to offer." Alan sips at his beer, too. "And we can never depend on Tom to be here when we need him." He discards three. Takes three.

"What did you say his name was? Jarod?" Fred sits up straight in his chair. "Yeah, it'd be nice to have another player." He discards nothing. "But do you think he'd be comfortable? Wouldn't want him to be uncomfortable. Maybe we could just have a cookout. You know? Get to know him a little better? A cookout's neighborly."

"Neighborly?" Jim smirks.

"Yeah, neighborly. You know, welcoming him to the neighborhood. Seems that might be enough. No reason to push it."

"You know, Fred, I think you're afraid."

Fred humphs.

"Really, son." Jim takes to calling grown men son when he's feeling authoritative and sheriffly. "You might be the last true blue American alive in this town."

"What's that supposed to mean?"

"Puttin' up borders before you even know the man."

"Sure, whatever you say Jim."

"Gotta be careful with borders, Fred. They

don't keep you safe. You can put a fence around yourself, around your house, you can even put a fence around our poker game, Fred, but everyone's still looking in. They can see you."

"So, let 'em look."

Jim shakes his head.

"What now?"

"Did it ever occur to you, Fred, that no one really cares to look?"

"Then why do they want to come inside and play poker?"

"They don't. It wasn't Jarod who's asking. It's Alan who's asking."

Sam raises the ante and discards two. Takes two. "Does he even know how to play?" Sam asks.

Jim takes as breath. "Did you know how to play, Sam?"

"Just saying. Maybe he won't even want to play."

"All right. Then it can't hurt to ask."

"It's just that he's new to the area and it would feel weird having someone new in our group. It would be uncomfortable."

"For who?" Jim grins.

"Whom." Sam says then withers when Jim glares at him.

Fred puts his cards face down on the table. "Okay, I'll say it. If no one else at this table is going to say it. I'll say it. He's black."

164

Jim has a special smile for the gotchas. It was the same sort of smile he used to give them as kids when he had a must do idea, like catapulting Sam from his mother's rooftop to the neighbor's rooftop with an elaborate machination of giant rubber bands they'd bought from the five and dime. Jim plays three nines.

"I'm just saying that he's not from here, not one of us," Fred says.

"So?"

"What if... listen. With just us, we can say whatever we feel like and there's no harm done."

"It's not like anyone here's going to say something stupid, Fred."

"I know, but what if someone does. I mean what if someone says something that we don't know is racist but is and Jarod gets all upset and goes blabbing to his wife and his wife talks to her friends and before you know it, we're a group of racist KKK bigots who meet and play poker and burn crosses on front lawns on the weekends. You're the sheriff, Jim. You'd think this would matter to you."

"Don't you think you're being a little paranoid?"

"No, I don't think I'm being paranoid. Paranoia is a belief based on an illogical set of expectations and fears. And this is just logic. It is possible that one of us might say something...rash and not even know it. How would you like it, Jim, if someone started spreading rumors that you're a racist?"

"That's not going to happen, Fred."

"But what if it did? What if it did happen? What would you do then? You've got an election to win next year."

"This isn't about me, Fred. This is about you."

"So what if it is? I have a practice to run."

"Three clients?"

"Five clients. Thank you. And they're five clients I'd like to keep."

"Listen, Fred. We all understand your reservations, but you can't be afraid of letting a guy play a game of cards because you're afraid to find out your racist and will lose your three clients."

"Five clients and I didn't say that I'm racist. When have I ever said anything racist? I'm not racist. I meant—"

"We all know what you meant."

"This isn't meeting new people you're talking about. This is bringing a complete stranger into our poker night." Fred waves his hands around to indicate the sanctity of the poker night and the card table and the tiffany lamp and beer tap and sideboard. He finishes by holding up one his cards with the naked brunette who has her legs bent back over her shoulders. She's smiling. "How are we going to find black cards?"

166

"What the hell do you mean?" Jim's upset now.

"Black ca ca ca…" Fred stops, swallows. "All our ca cards have white women on them. What if that offends him? You never know, it could offend him and then we'll need to get cards with black women, too. I don't know where to get cards with black women. Do you?"

The men all crack up laughing, except for Fred, who sits holding the card up like evidence of the end of the world. He stares at the laughing men as if they were a bunch of toddlers. He's pissed now.

Jim calms himself. "I don't think we'd have to do that, Fred."

"Okay, then let me remind you about high school and the district game and that girl Alan had the hots for, and how we almost got our heads knocked in. You want that to happen again? You want to bring him in here and disrupt our happy game."

"Jesus Fred."

Sam and Alan explode. Fred isn't laughing.

Jim stares Fred down. "Listen, that was a long time ago and we were all kids then."

Fred throws down his cards and crosses his arms.

"Okay, okay. We'll table it for now. How's that." Jim leans forward, puts a hand on Fred's elbow.

Fred nods, still agitated.

"Go on, pick up your cards."

The men sit in silence knowing that no one truly intends to invite Jarod. Not Fred or Sam or Jim or Alan. It's an exercise, a social narrative they've fallen into since the three of them got their asses kicked by the all black city defensive line for one's lust for a black cheerleader. And besides, asking a stranger into their game was like asking a girl into their secret club house.

By the time, Fred collects his chips and cards and has them all put away, because it would never occur to Fred that he could just leave the table and go upstairs and wait for them all to leave, he's visibly shaking. They wait for the "Thanks for the fucking good time," then they leave Fred at his door. Sam nods and gets into his car. Jim offers to drive Alan home and Alan says yes then sits in the cruiser and grabs the twisty tie from his pocket and molds it around his index finger then his middle finger. He will wait for the moment when he'll say, "You didn't need to do that," and Jim will answer, "I know. I feel kind of bad about it."

Shadow Spots

It is still with her, the water like silk and fireworks, fireflies drifting over long, warm grass.

The memory moves in partial detail. It plays in clips of scratched film between reel changes. She closes eyes for a more focused view behind dark lids, but she cannot grasp the whole of any one thing, like floating items in pool water — a plastic tube, a brown twig, a thin, tanned arm that might be a water snake though it is really too thick, and how many water snakes swim in chlorine anyway?

They float along easily, the items, overlaid with shadow spots. Hazy blur shapes in dark spaces. One spot resembles a giant bumble bee and it moves in the same lazy path as the tube and the arm that could be a water snake. It snaps from one spot to another. It doesn't matter which of the items the girl tries to study — the tube, twig, head of the snake — the bumblebee shifts with her. It is the detail the girl learns to hate, not the shadow spot, because the details are what she is deprived of, It is her biggest fear, missing details.

Sometimes her arms still ache from the

thrashing. Her body remembers; even now, her chest tightens. The pool and water are clear, as are her mother's red fingernails, the black bathing suit, the rust red hair, all in view, though the girl cannot see the color of her own suit. Shadow spots. The length of her body dissipates in the motion of the water, churning from clawing fingers at the surface while she breathes in chlorine air and water, tastes chemical in the back of her throat. A boy's hand is on top of her head, pushing her under the water. Certainly, the boy does not mean to drown her.

She cannot see the boy's face or remember his name, though they played all afternoon. He has become only a hand and a pair of legs that hang over the edge of the pool deck. His feet and calves dangle, cut off at the surface. He lets her up, periodically, and she catches her breath, mumbles incoherent water words before the boy pushes her back down again. His laughter is sharp then muted as the girl dies. It is enough to think one's death, sometimes.

When her mother grabs her arm, the water has already turned black, sparkling, spinning in circles, like middle school and suffocation games in the basement of a friend's house, birthday cake and ice cream. Pounding heartbeats turn to suggestions. *Don't struggle.* The black water moves

170

gently, holds her legs with soft pressure, not like her mother's grip on her arm. The water isn't altogether bad.

When her mother pulls-jerks the girl out of the water and over the pool edge, her voice is low. Everyone has stopped talking and they're staring as the girl. Her vision returns to her like shadow figures in a corrugated tunnel.

"What's wrong with you?" her mother says when they are away from the crowd, out of earshot. "I thought you were dying."

"I couldn't breathe." The girl coughs, tries to bring a hand to my mouth.

Her mother clenches the hand down and holds it at the girl's side.

"The boy, he was pushing me—" The girl coughs again. The pool water is still clearing from her lungs. With a free hand, she wipes dribbles of water as they fall from her nose. The water is red, and her mother stares at the hand, as if it has defied her, and so the girl lets the hand drop on its own this time.

"Don't ever do that again. I don't know what I'd do if anything happened to you."

The girl pretends that her mother said the last words before the first or all on their own. It helps to reorder her mother's sentences sometimes.

"I'm sorry," the girl says.

"Really?" Her mother pulls at the still wet arm, marches the girl through the hotel lobby,

171

back to the room, long red fingernails pushing into the girl's flesh, not hard enough to make a mark. They never do.

The girl sits on the couch while her mother goes to the bathroom, disgusted, her mouth twisted so that the lines on her face show more than usual and the girl takes her mother's disgust as if it has seeped out and onto the floor. The girl sops it up like spilt milk and throws it into herself.

I'm sleepy, the girl thinks, but knows better than to lie down.

In time, the girl wonders what her mother is doing in the bathroom, the door is shut for so long. It has become another shadow spot, the door, hiding more details and the girl is angry with her mother for hiding.

Quietly, she sits on the hotel room couch and blows the last of the pool water from her nose. There is more blood. She replays the incident in her mind, wondering how she might have done it better, avoided the embarrassment. Then she thinks: You stupid girl. Why didn't you just swim away?

Rae Bryant lives in the Washington D.C. area. Her work appears in *Puerto del Sol*, *Gargoyle Magazine*, *BLIP Magazine* (formerly *Mississippi Review*), *Opium Magazine*, *Caper Literary Journal* and *Foundling Review*, among other journals. She is a VCCA Fellow and a graduate of the M.A. in Writing program at Johns Hopkins University, where she was named Outstanding Graduate in Fiction. In 2011, she was awarded a fellowship to write and teach in Florence, Italy at the JHU Conference on Craft. Rae is currently finishing a novel. *The Indefinite State of Imaginary Morals* is her first book of fiction.

Made in the USA
Charleston, SC
19 September 2011